Love Is An Octopus

Zhauna Alexander

a *slipstream* book

Copyright © 2003

Tesseract Books and The Books Collective acknowledge the ongoing support of the Canada Council for the Arts for our publishing programme. We also acknowledge the assistance of the Edmonton Arts Council.

Editor for Press: Timothy J. Anderson.
Cover design by Anna Coe
Cover photo by Lee Anne Pellerin
Page design and typography by Ana M. Anubis of Ingénieuse Productions, Edmonton.
Printed by Priority Printing Ltd., Edmonton.

The text was set in Adobe's *Hiroshige*, designed in 1986 by Cynthia Hollandsworth of AlphaOmega Typography, Inc. The typeface was originally commissioned for a book of woodblock prints by the great nineteenth-century Japanese artist Ando Hiroshige, whose work influenced many Impressionist artists. The typeface has a gentle calligraphic flair that creates an interesting page of text as well as elegant headlines. The headlines are set in Fontek's *Twang*; section dividers are from Image Club's *Mini Pics Lil Fishies* collection.

Published in Canada by Slipstream Books, an imprint of
    The Books Collective
    214-21, 10405 Jasper Avenue
    Edmonton, Alberta T5J 3S2.
    Telephone (780) 448-0590   Fax (780) 448-0640

National Library of Canada Cataloguing in Publication Data

Alexander, Zhauna, 1973-
  Love is an octopus / Zhauna Alexander.

ISBN 1-895836-99-9

I. Title.
PS8551.L4736L68 2003   C813'.54   C2003-911262-4

This book is dedicated to my editor,
Timothy J. Anderson.

Deep thanks to my parents
and
Candas Jane Dorsey.

Note from the Editor

A woman in black S&M gear is standing on the street haranguing passersby to buy a ticket to Zhauna Alexander's latest *Fringe* show. Her sleek black hair frames a heart-shaped face with huge hazel eyes and a dazzling smile framed by sensuous lips. She promises the potential audience nudity. She promises lesbian sex. She promises a raunchy theatrical experience. She is a spike-heeled dominatrix porn fantasy made flesh: sexy, aggressive, and looking for action.

Beside her is an earnest-looking young woman in black slacks, a black long-sleeved turtleneck, and thick-framed glasses. She is as beautiful as the actress, but looks more like a political agitator. She is also screaming "Sex! Nudity!" and telling everyone the tickets are selling fast. She holds aloft a poster which features a photograph of the other woman — naked save for an "X" of duct tape over each of her beautiful breasts, and a gas mask. The earnest young woman wears trendy thick-soled shoes. She is a writer.

The tickets sell out. The house is full when the lights go down and the play begins. The language is stark and intense, the images cartoon-like and frightening. By the time the actress dons the gas mask and bares her breasts, the audience understands that they are not seeing pornography. They are seeing the work of a woman who explores huge issues: depression, addiction, redemption, danger. The media critics don't know what to make of this discomfiting satirical amalgam of *Disney*, *Brecht* and *Hefner*. The men who wanted sexploitation are baffled. The audience got what they were promised, and they're not sure they like it.

Along with the warnings of nudity, sex and foul language, there should have been a warning that the play would stimulate thought, deal with issues, and wrestle with content.

Now, a novel. Love is difficult enough for "normal" people. For those suffering from mental illness, emotional disorders, or childhood trauma, the search for love is full of danger. In this novel, Amelia Blue befriends her readers and takes them on a glass-bottomed boat ride, where we can watch her navigate her history and her manic-depressive condition (Amelia prefers the term "manic-depression" to "bipolar") as she struggles to find her place in the complex and shifting ocean.

These eight chapters cut through Amelia Blue's tentacled Gordian knot of love with the precision of neurosurgery. Beneath the surface ripples of humour, beneath the reefs of edginess lies an inky cloud of disturbed longing and desire. Zhauna Alexander explored

Amelia Blue's relationships with a writer's ruthlessness. Some of her observations continue to surprise and touch me even after working on the project for two years.

Love is an Octopus adds to an already impressive body of work: experimental films, gonzo Fringe plays, collaborations with musicians, and Ms. Alexander's previous books.

Beginning writers often ask me what it takes to get published. I would recommend they take Zhauna Alexander as their example. Be brilliant. Have something to say. Write your passion. Learn your craft. Promise them: "Nudity! Foul language! Sex!" Don't tell them they'll have to think. Get a sexy actress in high heels and duct tape to hawk your books.

Timothy J. Anderson, Editor

CHAPTER 1

Mama

I'm small like my Mama. People think I'm pretty. They don't know I want to be a fish.

Most of all, I want to be inside Mama again. It seems all my troubles began when I left Mama's body, when I was separated from Mama.

When people ask me how long I've been depressed, I say "Ever since I was born."

My Mama calls me "Amelia Blue" because I was born blue. Blue because Mama's umbilical cord was tied in a knot. Blue because my brain didn't get enough oxygen.

It could've been worse than manic depression. It could've been brain damage. Like Dr. Hill's son.

Mama says I cried a lot. Always wanted more milk. Mama breast fed me for two years. I clung to her like an octopus.

I still cling to Mama.

People think Mama and I are sisters. But we're more than sisters. More than twins. Mama and I are the same person. Except I'm a fish.

The doctor severed only one cord, the one he could see. The other one, the ghostly one, can stretch stretch stretch.

Once, I went to Calgary. The cord stretched all the way to Calgary. I was afraid. So very afraid it would tear. But it didn't.

Maybe I could go to Japan. But Japan is far far far. I want to be near Mama. I'm happiest near Mama. Except I'm never happy.

Mama and I share the same heart. The Wolf broke mine and Mama's heart.

One day, Mama and I wished The Wolf was dead. One day, we wished. Am I bad for wishing? Are Mama and I bad?

Then Mama's cousin phoned. She said The Wolf dropped dead. Out of the blue. No one knew why.

I wondered if Mama and I had killed The Wolf. Killed him with our wishing. Maybe Mama and I were witches.

I felt sad. Mama felt sad. We cried a river, even though The Wolf was bad bad bad.

I shouldn't cry. Mama and I shouldn't cry after what The Wolf did. I'm crying because Mama's crying. Mama's crying because I'm crying. I'm crying because I'm a fish.

I put my hand on Mama's belly. I tell her I was happy inside. Mama says she was happy too.

My depression is like mud. Thick and brown. And it sticks to me like mud.

People say I'm pretty. But they are afraid to get closer because I'm covered with mud. Thick and brown mud.

"It's unfortunate such a pretty girl is covered with mud," they think. If it were not for the mud, they'd love her.

Mama always made me shower and dress up to go to the doctor. I felt ridiculous in my freshly ironed blouse and my black dress pants. I didn't think the doctor would believe I was depressed.

I wanted to be dirty. I wanted to be "Smelly Melly". I wanted to go in my sweats. Mama wouldn't let me.

When I tried group therapy, Mama bought me a beige suit especially for the occasion. On the first day, the doctor was late and everyone ended up thinking I was the doctor.

I don't want to write. I hate writing. I write because I have to. It's the only thing I'm good at, the only way I can make money besides prostitution.

My books aren't selling well. I tell people money doesn't matter to me, but this is bullshit.

There are people who live to write. They write every spare moment they get. They carry a journal with them everywhere they go. They love writing. Francis is one of these people. I'm not. And because I'm not, I feel guilty.

I started telling people I was a writer when I was twenty. Mama said I wasn't a "real" writer until I got published. But I knew a girl that called herself a writer because she owned a magnetic poetry kit. Stick a few adjectives together and you're Margaret Atwood.

Wanting to be a writer when you're twenty is like wanting to be a rock star when you're twelve.

At first Mama didn't take my writing seriously. Mama wanted me to learn French and become a stewardess. Mama thought being a stewardess was glamorous. All that traveling, the uniforms, being around pilots. Mama thought pilots were sexy.

I think Mama liked the idea of saying to people, "Today, my daughter is in Singapore," or "Next week my daughter will be in Morrocco."

But after John F. Kennedy Jr. died, Mama became afraid of flying. With all the terrorism going on, she was glad I was a writer.

After I got published, Mama became my number one supporter. Now she's always telling me to write. Even on days I'm so depressed I can't brush my teeth. She does this out of love.

Mama was the one who bought me a computer, who made it easier to write. When I spilled some Diet Coke on the keyboard, she yelled at me. Out of love.

I'm lucky to have such a Mama. I'd like to dedicate a book to her, but she would be embarrassed because I use the word "fuck" a lot. Like now.

Mama begs me not to tell people I'm crazy. Mama says "crazy" is a bad word. With that awful "z" that drags on. Like in "lezzzbian". The worst thing you can be is a "crazzzy lezzzbian".

But it's too late. I've already told all my friends and about five hundred strangers.

I'm not sure why. Maybe because when you're crazy, saying "I'm crazy" makes you feel better. And you want to tell everyone like you're pregnant. "I'm crazy! I'm crazy! I'm fucking crazy!!!"

But I'm better now. So I don't tell people I'm crazy any more. I just tell them I'm manic-depressive.

Mama says this is still bad. That people don't have to know I'm manic-depressive. That she doesn't say, "Hi, I'm Mama, I'm diabetic," when she meets people.

I explain to Mama that manic-depression is the core of me. The centre. All that is good and bad comes from it. Without it, I am nothing.

One day, Mama and I are in a bookstore. Mama wants to buy me a book.
I pick *The Bell Jar* by Sylvia Plath.
Later, I tell Mama Sylvia Plath killed herself.
Mama is angry. She is afraid this book will push me over the edge.
I tell Mama people don't kill themselves because of books. Mama says she hopes no-one kills themselves because of my books.
I laugh at Mama and ask her to write an inscription.
She writes: Next time, I pick the book.

I changed psychologists as frequently as I changed lovers.
All of my psychologists were tall, like giants, and most of them wore spectacles and had a goatee. Like Sigmund Freud.
I hated them. They asked me all these stupid questions. I'd sit in a chair and repeat "I feel like shit" over and over. Sometimes, I gave them the finger.
They probed deeper and deeper. To get to the root. They wanted to know more about my childhood, about The Wolf, my lesbian love affair with X. I told them I was a blue baby. This wasn't enough for a psychologist but it would be enough for a psychiatrist.
This probing felt like a violation, a rape. I finally realized that the tall men in my dreams were these psychologists. They were the intruders in my basement.
Psychologists charge around eighty dollars an hour. Papa would be angry when I'd come home no different than when I left. It's as if he expected that his signing a cheque would magically transform me into a happy well-adjusted girl.
Poor Papa spent three thousand dollars on a woman who believed that there was nothing wrong with me.
The waiting list was long. Like a line up to get into a Marilyn Manson concert. Papa was sure glad when I got accepted by a psychiatrist. In Canada, the cost for a psychiatrist is covered. But one has to be truly ill to get accepted by a psychiatrist.
So when Dr. Hill accepted me, we celebrated not only because it was free but because it was official: I was mentally ill.

If I die tomorrow, what I'd miss most is watching films with Mama.

Mama and I've seen *Damage* about thirty times. We think Jeremy Irons is sexy. When his son falls over the staircase, Mama and I cry.

Our favourite line is, "Damaged people are dangerous. They know they can survive."

Mama and I are the same person except I'm bad bad bad and Mama's good good good. Good to the bone.

I think Mama is like Jesus. I don't think she's ever done a bad thing in her life. Mama tells me never to compare anyone with Jesus. That there was only one Jesus.

In kindergarten, Mama was the only Mama who was there all the time.

When I was older, she walked me to school and made my lunch every day. When I'd open my lunchbox there'd be a note that said "I love you" or "You're special" or "Don't be depressed."

Dr. Hill thinks Mama is the best Mama in the world. And everyone is always telling me how charming, funny and interesting she is. Even people who've just spoken to her on the phone.

I wish I was like Mama. They say a girl grows up to be just like her Mama, but I'm not charming or funny or interesting. And I have ugly legs.

I don't like myself much. Especially the fat. Ten pounds of it. Mama says women with excess fat on their thighs and bum are blessed. That it's easier to love a woman with defects.

When I tell Mama about the woman at the mall with bumps all over her skin, Mama says we're terrible for going on the way we do about our weight and our legs. That we should be beaten. Killed.

Mama's right. Mama's always right. I'm lucky to have a Mama who's always right.

Mama says I can live with her as long as I want. She says we can grow old together. That's good, because I don't know what I'd do without Mama. There is no me without Mama.

When I'm sixty, Mama will be eighty. When I'm eighty, Mama will be a hundred.

We'd live a simple life. In a small house. We'd have a patio, where we'd have our espressos. And there would be a swing. How Mama and I love swings. We'd also have a beautiful garden, an apple tree, and a lilac tree.

Lilacs smell so nice. Papa always brings Mama lilacs in the summer. Not only are they Mama's favourite, they don't cost a thing if you pick them in a park or from someone's bush when they're not looking.

Mama says she'd do all the cooking and cleaning if I support us with my writing. I don't know how much cleaning a hundred year old woman can do.

Mama thinks writing is the perfect profession for me because I can work when I want to. If I feel ill in the morning, I can write in the afternoon or in the evening or next week or in six months. And when I acquire enough readers, I don't have to write at all. I can sit back and do absolutely nothing while the money from the sales of my previous books keeps rolling in. I can be a crazy old woman and never have to worry about money. Mama and I can be crazy and old together. Except Mama can never be crazy.

I hope Mama and I die together. In our sleep.

We will have grave plots next to each other. I want the right one. I'm a righty.

If Papa is good, he can live and die with us. And when we run out of lilacs, he can supply us.

My father's father was a Father. He broke his vows, left the church, and married a Chinese woman.

My Papa was the youngest son. He rejected his Papa's Catholicism and adopted his Mama's Buddhism.

My Papa's Mama was a good woman. Her man left her for a whore. A white whore. After Papa's Mama bore Papa's Papa eight children. Eight is supposed to be a lucky number for the Chinese.

People say my Mama looked just like me. Except her hair was lighter. Bleached by the sun. She was a virgin. My Papa was a map maker. They met on a boat. If it had hit an iceberg, I wouldn't have been born.

Shortly after my parent's love affair blossomed, Papa had to leave. He was gone a year. But he wrote and reassured Mama that distance was the only thing keeping them apart.

Mama has a treasure chest full of postcards from all over the world. She says she fell in love with my Papa's words. Maybe someday someone will fall in love with mine.

Mama could write poetry if she wanted to. She chooses not to. I've never asked her why.

When I think of what an artist is, I think of a nineteen year old Jean-Michel Basquiat sleeping in a cardboard box. I don't sleep in a cardboard box. I sleep on a queen size orthopedic mattress and I live with my parents. I'm thirty years old and I still live with my parents.

Mama washes and irons my clothes. Mama cooks for me. Mama cleans up after me. Papa scolds me. He says I'm manic-depressive, not handicapped. Every week I say I will do these things, but I never do.

My editor says a lot of child prodigies grow up to be ordinary. I wish I was ordinary. But Buddy says I wouldn't be me then.

Mama and Papa never treated me like I was mentally ill. Sometimes, I wish they had. I remember yelling at them, "I'm not normal."

Papa says despair will not kill you. But I think he's wrong.

Papa also says that suffering breeds art. That all great artists suffer. Knowing that Sylvia Plath and Virginia Woolf suffered from the same malady as me is comforting. Knowing that they killed themselves is not.

The Chinese believe that energy must flow freely throughout the body to maintain good health. When energy is blocked, disease occurs.

Ovarian cancer runs on Papa's side. I'm afraid I will get ovarian cancer. So I masturbate to keep the energy flowing.

I masturbate only for health reasons. I don't find masturbation sexy. Unless, of course, someone is watching.

I think of awful things when I masturbate. Of men wearing black ski masks. Men tying me up and raping me. Like a scene out of *Clockwork Orange*.

I am drawn to violence. Dr. Hill says it's because The Wolf was so gentle. Had he been rough it would've been the other way around.

Mama says I should stop writing poetry. That I should write a novel. About love. Like Marguerite Duras. I tell Mama I know nothing of love.

Marguerite Duras is dead. She didn't die too long ago. I think she was in her eighties. Dr. Hill thinks I could make it into my eighties. He says he could see me writing books for the rest of my life.

The only problem is, I hate writing now. When I call my editor and tell him I hate writing, he says I'm a real writer now.

How much of Marguerite Duras is in her books? How much of me is in mine? Maybe there is no X. No Francis. No Vincent. Maybe my Mama died when I was little. Maybe I'm fucking with you. Maybe I like fucking with you. Maybe I like to fuck.

When someone asked Reinaldo Arenas why he wrote (after he got out of prison), he said "Revenge".

When a journalist asked me what my message was, I said I didn't have a message, unless "Fuck you" was my message. I called my editor and asked him if "Fuck you" can be a message. He said yes. So I called back the journalist and said "Fuck you" was definitely my message.

After all, writing about someone can be the ultimate fuck you. Anyone who's screwed you over, you can screw back tenfold. Publicly.

I know X and Francis and Vincent will read my books. Out of curiosity. I hope my words sting. I hope I hurt them. I suppose this makes me a sadist.

I went through a forgiving phase. Forgiving X, Francis, Vincent, The Wolf. I stopped being pissed off. But my writing suffered. My editor said I had lost my edge. So, I became pissed off again.

My poor editor. I call him every month and tell him I'm going to slash my wrists in the bath. The right way: up and down. He just says, "Finish the book first."

When I call and tell my editor my writing is killing me, he says the sales of my books will go up when I'm dead.

People think being a writer is a respectable profession, but I think we're just whores.

I think when someone reads your writing it's like copulation between the reader and the writer.

If you only write for yourself, it's like masturbation.

If someone reads your writing for free, then you're a slut.

If someone pays to read your writing, it's like prostitution. And prostitution, dear reader, is the oldest profession in the world.

I hate it when I'm in a coffee shop writing and someone asks me if I'm doing my homework. Then I have to explain that I'm a lot older than I look and that I'm writing a novel.

Then they ask me what I write about. I hate it when they ask me this. I don't want to tell people I write about depression and fucking. So I say I write about love. This usually satisfies them.

I say the same to my Mama's Mama. I can't say "I write about fucking" to my Mama's Mama, a seventy year old woman who was raised a strict Catholic. So when I say "I write about love", my Mama's Mama replies: "That's wonderful, child."

I wish beautiful young men and women would ask me about my writing. Only fat ugly old people do. Maybe fat ugly old people read more than everyone else. Who knows, maybe one day a million fat ugly old people will buy my book and make me very rich. Then I will be grateful to all those fat ugly old people.

Papa told me I was a poet instead of telling me I was ill.

Papa has his black moods too. Sometimes I wish he wasn't my father. Sometimes I wish Dr. Hill was my father.

Papa says awful things. That he wants to be in a car accident, that he wants to die. I remember him saying this when I was little, too. Maybe he wouldn't have said it if I wasn't a prodigy. Or if he knew I was clinically depressed.

Sometimes I think I inherited my depression from my Papa's side. Not because I was born a blue baby. But Papa has always maintained that I'm not depressed because of his family. That no-one is depressed on his side. Not even him.

According to Papa, if anyone's depressed, it's on Mama's side. The Wolf was on my mother's side. Therefore perversion, immorality, and insanity run on Mama's side. If I inherited my illness, if I had anyone to blame, it was Mama's family.

Now two of Papa's siblings are on antidepressants. Mama says she always suspected they were depressed. Mama says it doesn't matter who carries the genes for depression. It's no-one's fault I am ill. Blaming someone doesn't change anything.

Mama also says Papa would be a different man if he weren't in debt. I know there is truth to this, but I still wish Papa was on antidepressants.

Instead of arguing over whose family I inherited my illness from, Mama and Papa went with Dr. Hill's theory. The blue baby theory was safer. And it stuck.

I wasn't much different as a child than I am now. I used to play a little game with myself. I used to pretend to pass out and be unconscious. I would let my body go limp and lie still for as long as I could. I was good at this game. Once, the school called an ambulance because I appeared to be unconscious for half an hour.

In fifth grade, I was tested for my I.Q. My teacher told my parents I was a prodigy. And that they could put me in university next year instead of the sixth grade. But Mama and Papa decided that a normal childhood that was good enough for their two other children would be good enough for me. Besides, they were worried I'd get kidnapped or raped or killed.

Soon after, a strange man began to follow me around and photograph me. Mama called the police. It was the first time a police car was ever parked in front of our house.

After I gave a description, the police told my parents that the same man had been seen with two other little girls right before they had gone missing.

From that day on, Mama became ten times the mother hen that she had been. She never let us out of her sight. She did everything she could to prevent the worst from happening. But it happened anyway. Right under her nose. Poor poor Mama.

When puberty hit, I became a terror. I abused Mama and my sisters. I hit them, scratched them, bit them, and pulled their hair. I was like the possessed girl in *The Exorcist*. Except my head couldn't go all the way around.

In a moment of rage, I ripped all my photos of my sisters. Mama didn't get mad because she had already gotten mad when I drew devil's horns and goatees on them.

Papa threatened to put me in a juvenile detention home. He even drove me by one to scare me. I just said, "Go ahead."

There was a lot of shouting in our house. The neighbours must've heard. Maybe they thought Papa was hurting us; that Papa was a bad man. But the noise, the terrible noise, was coming from me.

I told Mama I wished she had never given birth to me. Mama said if she could she would be depressed for me.

I secretly hoped someone would kill me so I wouldn't have to do it myself. So I wouldn't have to go to hell.

By high school, I was so fucked up I dropped out and completed my courses by correspondence.

The people I grew up with wondered what had happened to the girl who won the Grade Nine Science Fair. Some people were glad I was struggling. There will always be people who want to see you fail.

I wondered too. I had been brilliant for so long. How could I adjust to being anything less?

I got my high school diploma two years later than my friends. I wanted to go to university, but now my marks were too low. I blamed Mama and Papa every day. "I could've had a Ph.D," I would say.

I managed to enroll in a community college. I was an English major and I wrote for the school paper. But by second semester, I had a nervous breakdown and had to be hospitalized. Again, some people must've been happy.

Dear reader, you know you've hit rock bottom, when they don't let you shave your legs with even the dullest razor. When they check on you every half hour at night, which makes it impossible to masturbate. When they make you sing Kumbaya every day. And believe you me, you will sing motherfucking Kumbaya a thousand times if you want to get out of the hospital.

And then there are the crazy people. No matter how crazy you think you are, the people in the psych ward will scare you. I remember a man who thought Michael Jackson was communicating with him through his *Free Willy* video.

Who would've thought I'd meet Dr. Hill, my cute little blue-eyed saviour, in that hell hole.

Dr. Hill is different from the other doctors. He wears outrageous Hawaiian shirts instead of suffocating turtlenecks. And he's short.

Maybe Dr. Hill and I clicked because he was a child prodigy too. Dr. Hill went to university when he was only twelve.

Or maybe it's because he's eccentric. He never wears socks. Even in winter.

But I think it was because his son was also born a blue baby.

Unfortunately, Dr. Hill's son is "slow". Who would have guessed a genius would have a "slow" child? I'm lucky compared to Dr. Hill's son. At least I can read and write.

Dr. Hill has other tragedies too. His father died when he was only six. And his brother has cancer.

Dr. Hill can't help those closest to him. Instead, he helps anorexics, bulimics, compulsive obsessives, schizophrenics, and me.

Mama and I share the same heart. Except Mama has a hole in her side. Poor Mama lost her only brother.

She had a dream the night before. She saw everything as if through a window: the storm, the bridge, Manuel's silver Mercedes Benz losing control, Manuel's neck breaking. Mama was already dead when the phone rang.

Manuel's wife howled like a wounded animal.

Mama's limbs gave out. She fell like a doll, scraping her forehead against the corner of the kitchen table.

When I saw Mama lying lifeless on the floor, I thought I'd fall too. She lay still for minutes that seemed like hours. How striking she looked with the red gash on her forehead. I admired her high cheekbones, her full lips, and arched eyebrows. I thought myself pretty as I stared down at her.

Mama didn't speak for ten days. I thought she would never speak again.

There was no sleeping either. Just doors opening and closing. And shuffling from room to room.

"Manuel, Manuel," Mama whispered. But no answer would come.

Afterwards Mama was never the same. Manuel was a touchy subject. Mama would become breathless at the mere mention of his name. Apart from The Wolf, Manuel's death was Mama's greatest tragedy.

I didn't spend much of my childhood with Manuel, but I too felt a loss. Handsome, clever, and charming, he was the perfect male specimen. The man I would model my lovers after for the rest of my life.

When I ask Mama if she thinks I'm bisexual she says, "No, sweetie, I think you're just perverted."

My sisters believe that you're born gay, that it's an illness. But that you choose to be bisexual.

My sisters think I am this way because I'm an artist, but sometimes they make me feel like a criminal.

As for Papa, he says I haven't met the right man yet.

What can I say about my sisters? They were normal girls with normal lives. The only thing that wasn't normal was their crazy sister, me. They avoided me as much as possible. This wasn't hard because they were older, so we went to different schools and had different friends.

My sisters never brought anyone home. They were too afraid I'd make a scene and embarrass them.

We didn't look like sisters. And we didn't act like sisters. Sometimes I felt like I was living with two strangers.

One of my sisters was a swimmer. How I admired her. Swimmers have wonderful shoulders. I wanted to be a swimmer, but I could barely float.

My other sister sang in a choir. She had a lovely voice. She could've been something, but she got married right away and had kids.

Soon enough, my sister the swimmer followed in her footsteps.

My sisters and I call each other at Christmas and on each other's birthdays. Like proper sisters. But that's about it.

The truth is, I hate my sisters. Because they're happy and I'm not. I want everyone to be ill and suffer like me.

So many times I have cursed them and their children.

When my sisters got married, I cried at their weddings. But my tears were for me, because it wasn't me walking down the aisle.

Mama says that deep down my sisters and I love each other a lot. If one of us needed a kidney, we'd give her ours.

I'm scared of lesbians. I always thought all lesbians were butchy and hairy. That they were like men except without penises.

If I'm going to be with a man, he had better have a penis, and a big one for that matter.

Mama says all women are trouble, that women are bitches. That X was a bitch.

My editor thinks I should find a nice couple. That I shouldn't settle for one when I can have both.

The pathetic thing is, you'd think I would have twice the chance of finding someone. Yet I am alone. I haven't had a lover for three years. And on Saturday night, instead of a hot date, I stay home and masturbate.

Tall men. Tall houses. Serpents.

The dream is always the same. Tall men fondle me in tall houses full of serpents. I'm the same age I am now. But because these men are so tall, maybe eight or nine feet tall, I feel like a child.

The dream is always the same. No bones, no blood. Just flesh. Dr. Hill says they're phantoms.

My Mama and Papa are in the dream. They help me bury the remains. Then, we move to L.A.

All of my friends have a variety of dreams. But I keep having the same one. Buddy thinks I should reduce the amount of cheese in my diet.

I think if I weren't an artist I'd be a criminal.

I think a lot of criminals should've been artists.

Adolph Hitler was an artist before he became a criminal.

Now, I have to take antidepressants and antipsychotics three times a day, like meals. And tranquilizers whenever I need them, which is all the time.

I have to get my blood tested every two weeks. I always have needle marks on my arm. People might think I'm a heroin addict.

I see Dr. Hill every week. We talk for half an hour. It's always the same thing: I tell him I feel depressed, that I'm fat, that I want to kill myself.

Dr. Hill says the same things too: that I'm a good person, that I'm not fat, and that I need to be more patient.

I love Dr. Hill like a daughter loves her father.

I've never met Dr. Hill's son, but I think of him often. I feel like we're connected because we were both blue babies. Every week, I ask Dr. Hill how he is. And at Christmas, I buy him a present.

I'm not like my sisters. I can't have children.

Dr. Hill says if I stopped taking my meds, I would probably have a miscarriage. If I got pregnant and continued taking my meds, I would probably have a deformed child. If I didn't have a miscarriage or a deformed child, if I had indeed inherited my illness, then my child could be manic-depressive too.

I am not going to gamble. My luck so far sucks.

Besides, the good news is I will be spared labour pains and stretch marks. I have enough stretch marks already.

And because I will never have a child with my body, I felt I would never become a real woman. That I would stay a girl forever.

Mama said if she was any younger, she would have a child for me. She'd give me a child. This child, her child, could call me "Mama," she said. But Mama is already in her fifties, and this would be a gamble as well.

As for my sisters, they didn't make me this offer.

I barely see my sisters' children. Probably because I'm depressed and bisexual and I cursed them.

My sisters have beautiful children. Sometimes, I pretend they are my own. I squeeze their cheeks and give them candy and money. I try not to love them too much.

When I look back on my happiest day, as close to happiness as I was going to get, I think of one rainy day in my childhood when Mama, Papa, and my sisters went fishing.

I was the only one who caught a fish that day. We didn't even eat it; we let it go because we felt sorry for it.

I became one with the lake that day.

This is what must have happened: my soul must have fallen in love with the lake and joined it. And when my body returned home, my soul remained with the lake. Except it was still with Mama, a part of Mama, the same as Mama.

It was then that I knew I wanted to be a fish, was a fish, always will be a fish no matter how many incarnations.

After Mama and Papa had my sisters, they had hoped for a boy. But when I was born, they loved me just the same. And Papa raised me as his son.

He was proud of me that day at the lake. The day I caught the fish. He said I was his fisherman. Mama called me "Amelia Blue" but Papa called me "The Fisherman."

I wondered if maybe because Mama and Papa had wanted a boy, I was a boy, had a boy's soul. Maybe their hoping and wishing had changed me into a boy. Maybe Mama was a witch. Maybe I was something in between a boy and a girl. And maybe because I wasn't quite a boy or a girl, I became a fish.

Mama thought I was just experimenting with X. But Papa knew I loved her because she was a Pisces and I was still his son, The Fisherman.

I feel like I have been on more fucking drugs than Keith Richards. I can't remember what they were all called, only that most of them ended with –il or –yl. Mama has a list somewhere.

Every drug seemed to have a side effect. Some made my mouth too dry. Some increased my appetite. Some made my hands shake. Like lithium. Lithium really made my hands shake. Lithium wasn't good for me. People think every manic-depressive is on lithium, but this isn't true.

Anyway, I remember reading on one of the bottles of an antidepressant that a side effect was depression. How fucked is that?

I collected pills like some people collect stamps. I had so many different coloured ones, I thought I'd make myself a necklace.

When I get sick of being a guinea pig, I let Buddy sample my meds. He couldn't turn down free drugs.

You may not believe me, but I don't want to have any more lovers. I may be young to be making this kind of decision. I'm only thirty.

I've had many lovers, too many to count. I'd be embarrassed to tell you.

Most of them were strangers, strange men. I didn't know what films they liked to watch, what music they liked to listen to, or what books they liked to read. Some of them I didn't even know their names.

Maybe I'm a slut, but you wouldn't think that by the looks of me. By the looks of me, you would think I was a nice girl.

Maybe I don't want a lover because of the pills. Mama says this is better than being promiscuous. Mama worries about her daughter. She doesn't want her to get AIDS, herpes, hepatitis or bluekemia.

Dear reader, if you had to choose between wanting to fuck all the time and not wanting to fuck at all, which would you choose? I chose the latter. It's easier when your sex isn't always wet and throbbing and all you can think about are hands, cocks and mouths. There's more to life than hands, cocks and mouths.

Buddy thinks I'm depriving myself.

Papa still thinks I haven't met the right man yet.

Chapter 2
The Wolf

You never forget a wolf.

My eyes are wet because I will never forget. Mama's eyes are wet too. It's like looking into the mirror.

It took me ten years to figure out my wolf was a Wolf.

My Wolf had nice eyes. Kind eyes. Sometimes when I peered into them I saw a boy.

He was a handsome wolf, as often wolves are. But his fat disgusted me. Even though his face was pleasant, all I could think about was the fat.

Maybe The Wolf thought I wouldn't mind his advances because he had a handsome face. It wouldn't be like molestation. More like seduction. Like an affair.

Maybe because he had a handsome face, he thought I would be his mistress. His eight year old mistress.

In the long hot summer, he would walk around shirtless. All his fat hanging out. His fat was all in one area, his stomach. To me, he looked like a pregnant man. It just wasn't natural. It repulsed me.

I could talk about this fat forever. This fat stifled my childhood. Like a big pillow being pressed against my face. I couldn't breathe because of this fat. I was suffocating.

When I think of The Wolf, I think of two things: his fat and his hands.

He was always pawing me. His hands were always on my thighs, an inch away from my genitals. He would slowly follow the lines of my panties with his fingers. His hands would get closer and closer. When they were inside my underwear, I flinched like a fish and moved away. It was like a game. He wanted to see how far I would let him go.

Maybe if he had been thinner and younger (he was forty-four years older than me, dear reader) I wouldn't have been so disgusted. Maybe if he had been perfect like Manuel, I would've let him go further.

The Wolf was my shadow. I couldn't get away from him except to go to the bathroom. So, I pretended to have stomach aches. But after a while, not very long, he would knock, ask me questions, ask to come in.

I promised myself that I would never love someone like this, to never love them too much.

When The Wolf kissed me, he stuck his tongue in my mouth. No-one had ever kissed me like this. I was eight years old. I thought he was being silly. I laughed. He was funny to me.

He kept asking me to undress. He said he wanted to see how beautiful I was. This didn't sound strange. This made sense.

He begged me every day. "Please, I want to see how much your titties have grown. You'll do it if you love me." Then, he pretended to cry. He said I was making him sad.

I didn't want him to be sad. So I showed him my nipples that looked like mosquito bites.

Then, he asked me to take my pants off so he could see if there was any hair down there. But I was too shy.

His next request was to see me shower. He said he wanted to see if I was cleaning myself properly. He said I had to wash thoroughly down there.

This made sense too. But I was coughing in the middle of the night, fighting for breath in my sleep.

If I did what he asked, I felt bad. If I didn't do it, I felt bad too. I couldn't win.

The Wolf didn't touch my genitals, but his hands were so close, too close. It was not right. But because he didn't put his fingers inside me or make me perform fellatio on him, or rape me, I didn't think anything was happening.

When he gave up on the shower, he asked me to pee on some grass in front of him. He said it would help the grass grow. This made sense too. So I did it.

I peed in front of him many times. One day, he asked me to pee in his mouth. This seemed yucky.

Now, when I look back, I don't know if he really wanted me to urinate in his mouth or if it was his way to get me to let him perform cunnilingus on me.

So if this doesn't count, tell me, reader, how much damage do you think a grown man asking a child to urinate in his mouth can do?

At the time, I thought he was just being silly again. Why would someone want you to pee on them? Urine was yucky. Why would someone like that? Maybe he was joking.

The Wolf was a very serious man. I can still see him sipping his espresso and reading the newspaper. He was one of those people who read a newspaper from front to back.

The Wolf was interested in politics. In Blueland, everyone was interested in politics. Politics was as popular as sex. Every doctor had a political magazine in his office. And on the cover would be a naked woman. That's Blueland for you.

I drank coffee ever since I was a little kid. The Wolf didn't mind me drinking coffee. But he wouldn't let me smoke. He was a chainsmoker and figured his destiny was to die of lung cancer. But this would not be.

The Wolf and I would have our espressos together and he'd read to me how the country was falling apart and how the political leaders were to blame for ethnic problems.

I called The Wolf by his first name ever since I can remember. It was a bit weird, but everyone did.

The Wolf talked to me like I was on his level, like an intellectual. Maybe it wasn't my little girl's body he was attracted to but my ripe mind.

The Wolf taught me how to play chess. He was pleased when I beat him. He told everyone I was a genius. He was proud of me. And this felt good.

The Wolf wanted me to sleep in the same bed with him. He asked Mama. He said he wanted to be close to me because he loved me so much.

Mama said "No" without any thought or hesitation. She didn't know The Wolf was a wolf and that when he was asking to share a bed with her daughter, he was actually asking permission to rape her.

Now, Mama says she doesn't think The Wolf would've raped me. I think she's wrong. We will never know. We will stay up night after night wondering. But we'll never know.

The Wolf told me he wanted to adopt me, wanted me to live in Blueland with him. He offered to take me off Mama's hands, to protect me, comfort me, to drive away the demons so I wouldn't have anymore nightmares.

The problem though was, he was the demon. He was the fat and hands in my nightmares.

Blueland was far far far. On the other side of the world. We didn't visit The Wolf much. And when we did, Mama and Papa were there. Everyone saw but no one knew. Not even me.

There were no wolves in our family. There couldn't be. We weren't like that.

I have this feeling that if people knew who did what to me, they'd say I'm a liar or a lesbian or a whore. Maybe they'd say I wanted it to happen, because he was handsome. Maybe they'd say I flirted with him, led him on. Maybe they'd say I liked it.

Maybe a gang of men would seek me out and rape me to teach me a lesson. To prove what a whore I am.

Before The Wolf died, I fantasized about paying him a visit. We'd drink espressos on the patio. I would be sweet to him like I still loved him, like he didn't ruin Mama's and my life.When he wasn't looking, I'd pour some poison in his cup.

It would be a slow agonizing death. It would take days. He would suffer.

The Wolf hated doctors. He probably wouldn't let them take him to the hospital 'til the last minute, when it was too late.

It was a simple plan. No-one would know it was me.

If a man forces a woman to have intercourse with him, then it is rape. Anything else is not. Anything else is less than rape.

Rape is the worst thing that can happen to a woman. The worst thing that a man can do to her.

If The Wolf had raped me, then I could say, "Mama, he raped me." He would go to jail. It would be terrible, but I'd go into therapy and I would get over it somehow.

But because I wasn't raped, what does an eight year old say to her Mama?

My father says I was lucky I wasn't raped. My father is right, it would've been worse. But just because The Wolf's penis wasn't inside me doesn't mean I wasn't fucked.

At least if I was raped, things would be clearer, less confusing. I wouldn't have to analyze everything to death.

I didn't realize what had been done to me until I went into therapy.

The Wolf didn't do it to Mama, but because he did it to me and Mama and I are the same person, he might as well have done it to her. Mama and I hurt equally. Sometimes I think she hurts more.

Sometimes I feel as though it was me who ruined her life. If there was no me, maybe The Wolf wouldn't have been a wolf.

The Wolf didn't give my sisters candy and jewelry. He didn't take them to meet his mistress. I felt bad for my sisters. I used to ask The Wolf to buy them things. And he would, but only because I asked him to.

Everyone knew I was The Wolf's favourite, but my sisters weren't jealous.

I often wonder why it happened to me and not my sisters. After all, they were pretty.

I wish I wasn't the only one he did it to. I wish it had happened to someone besides me. Then I wouldn't feel so alone, so utterly alone. I could be certain. It could feel real. I could say, "Yes, this happened."

Maybe the ambiguity of this experience made me an ambiguous person. Maybe this is how I became a fish.

Maybe Mama is right. Maybe I turned to women, turned to X, because there was a wolf in my childhood.

There are lots of wolves out there. Lots of women with lots of wolves in their lives. I'm sure I'm not the worst case. Not even close to being the worst case. Of course not. I wasn't raped.

Some girls are raped or sodomized by their own fathers. Or are pregnant with their father's child. They give birth to a two headed baby. It's a horror out there. The world is a horror. I'm lucky. What happened to me was minor compared to those girls.

But I have a story. This is my story. It matters. I deserve to be heard.

Am I crazy because The Wolf was crazy?

No. I didn't get enough oxygen. I was born a blue baby. That's my story.

It's bad enough I'm crazy, but I don't want to be crazy because of him. I'd rather be consumed with my illness than with him. I don't want him to be the core, the centre.

But he's inside me, will always be. Even though he's dead. You see dear reader, he is in my blood.

Was The Wolf always a wolf or had he become one? And if so, what caused him to become one? Was it World War II? Was he raped?

Mama says he lost his daughter. She was four. Poor little girl died of pneumonia. Maybe this was the turning point.

Imagine a little coffin. I always thought little coffins were creepier than big ones. There was something unnatural, wrong about little coffins.

The Wolf had a picture of his dead daughter in the room where Mama and I slept. The Wolf said I looked just like his dead daughter, except for the hair. This disturbed me greatly. If The Wolf thought I looked like his daughter, reminded him of her, was he sexually attracted to her too? Did he molest her as well?

She was only four when she died. It's sick to molest an eight year old, but it's even sicker to molest a four year old.

When Papa told me about reincarnation, I began to wonder if perhaps I was The Wolf's daughter. And that's why The Wolf saw her in me.

I stared at his daughter's picture 'til the image was burned in my mind. I couldn't see the resemblance The Wolf saw. His daughter was much prettier than me.

Besides, I looked like a boy.

The Wolf hated homosexuals. I remember him making fun of his wife's cousin. Saying he was a "fag" and disgusting and sick in the head and that he deserved to be killed.

I don't think The Wolf was attracted to boys. My editor said he read somewhere that pedophiles don't care whether it's a boy or a girl. That when they're children, they're almost the same.

The Wolf would probably think I was disgusting if he knew I had slept with a woman. He would probably scold me. Isn't it funny how a sick person can think someone else is sick?

I wish I understood The Wolf, but Dr. Hill says I wouldn't want to be in The Wolf's mind.

This is my guess as to what happened, how The Wolf became a wolf. Maybe he loved his little daughter so much, he went crazy when she died. Then, I came along and he loved me so much, too much, that the line between natural love and unnatural love got fuzzy. He didn't know how to love anymore. When he lost the person he loved more than anyone in the world, he lost his mind and didn't know how to love. His thoughts and feelings and desires got all mixed up.

The Wolf was a loveable man, a nice man, a sweet man. It hurts even more because he was so nice and sweet. Had he been like Hitler, I could say, "Fuck him, he was an awful man, a sadist." The Wolf was a war hero, an intellectual, a generous man, a kind man. Besides smoking and having extramarital affairs, his only vice was being a child molester. Eventually, he would even quit smoking.

So who would believe me if I told them what The Wolf had done? Would you, dear reader?

This man had a wife and a mistress; his plate was full. And he could have any woman he wanted, even though he was fat. Why would he want a little kid?

Now I'll tell you the story about the kitten.

There was a stray kitten. I played with it every day. I came to love this kitten. It was gray with black stripes.

One day, the kitten disappeared. The Wolf told me someone had drowned her. I believed the wicked Wolf.

Ten years later, I found out he had lied. The kitten hadn't been drowned but taken across the river.

Everyone was always touching and squeezing her. This wasn't good for a little kitten. This was too much love. So someone took her across the river to start a new life. A life with less love.

I was happy that the kitten hadn't been killed. But I was sad too. Sad that The Wolf would intentionally hurt me like that. All those years I thought this cute little kitten that I loved had been drowned, murdered. Was this part of his game?

The Wolf played chess and cards and badminton with me. He was good to me in many ways. He bought me jewelry and gave me money. Like some men do for their wives or mistresses.

Not only was I maybe The Wolf's daughter in a past life, but maybe I was his lover in a past life too. Maybe in the life before this one, I was his daughter. And in the life before that, I was his wife. Who knows? Sometimes, I wish I had the answers. Other times, I hope I never do.

If The Wolf didn't molest his daughter, it's still sick that he thought I looked like her and molested me. Wouldn't that be like molesting her? Like molesting his very own daughter?

This is awful, that I have to think about these things, but if I stop thinking about them, I will turn into a zombie like The Wolf's wife. I will walk around doing things like I'm not there. I will be half dead.

The Wolf knew I loved orange soda pop. He bought a crate of it and put it in a dark creepy shed occupied by a fierce mother hen and her chicks.

I feared two things: the hen and The Wolf's hands. I remember him being behind me, his eager hands stroking my thighs.

I was hopelessly addicted to orange soda pop. So I went to the shed every day. And every day, he was behind me. I could feel his heavy breath.

I felt like the kitten must've felt. I wanted someone to take me across the river.

There was an outhouse in the chicken run and near the pigpens. No one used it. But The Wolf wanted me to use it. I didn't know why. The outhouse smelled awful. I didn't want to, but he insisted.

He stood in front of the outhouse, smoked a cigarette and listened to me pee and you-know-what. He acted like he was there for conversation, but he was there for something else.

Who would believe that a kind man, a handsome man with a good Mama and good brothers would do this? Who would believe me? Do you still believe me, dear reader?

Mama thinks maybe The Wolf was raped by men, by soldiers in World War II. Mama says The Wolf was only a little kid when he became a soldier. He was a war hero. His picture is up in some museum and he's been written about in some books. I guess you could say he's sort of famous.

Mama says awful things happen in wars. It is possible The Wolf was raped, sodomized and that was his root, why he became a wolf. When Mama told me this, I almost felt sorry for The Wolf. Maybe he was raped, sodomized, and that's why he hated homosexuals and was so repulsed by them.

The Wolf had a wonderful Mama. She was practically a saint. Mama and I loved her dearly. I don't know how such a good woman could give birth to a wolf.

I have a pair of gold earrings she gave me. She was a poor woman. But she saved her coins and bought me the gold earrings. I was going to give them to my daughter, but I will never have a daughter.

It was me who answered the phone when Manuel's wife called to tell us of The Wolf's Mama's death. And I was the one who had to tell Mama. It's hard to be the bearer of bad news.

Over five hundred people attended The Wolf's Mama's funeral. Everyone loved her. She was the most loved woman in the village.

The Wolf had two brothers. They were good like their Mama. They died around the same time. We cried buckets. How could a man have such a good Mama and such good brothers and be a wolf?

It's hard for me to wear those gold earrings The Wolf's Mama gave me. I loved her, but a part of me hates her for giving birth to The Wolf. It's not right to blame her. I know this. But I feel like she brought him into this world, brought his evil into this world and into my life. I'm angry at her for this, so I don't talk about her much.

When Mama mentions her, says she was a good woman, I nod and say, "Yes, she was a good woman." But I secretly resent her.

I love her for giving birth to two good sons, but I can't forgive her for the one bad son. That's the way it is.

The blouse was black, soft, cotton I think. It was my favourite.

I know The Wolf liked it. He asked me to wear it when he took me to meet his mistress.

A couple of days before we left Blueland, it went missing. I looked everywhere, but I couldn't find it. I remember yelling at Mama.

Now, I think The Wolf took it. I think he wanted to have something that belonged to me, to remember me by. This is sweet, almost romantic. He could've asked me. I would've let him have it.

What if he smelled it when he masturbated? Or what if he rubbed his you-know-what with it? Or what if he ejaculated onto it? Maybe I'm wrong, but is it too much to assume from a man that listens to a child do their business in an outhouse?

The Wolf wanted to adopt me. He asked Mama if I could stay in Blueland with him and go to school in Blueland. Mama laughed. She thought he was only half serious.

What would have happened to me had Mama let The Wolf raise me?

Yes, this is as sick as it can get. Not only was I being molested, I was being incested. But according to The Webster's dictionary, "sexual intercourse" would have to take place for it to be incest. So technically I wasn't "incested". According to the fucking dictionary.

All of my lovers have been thin. Some skeletal.

When I was a child, I fantasized about being abducted by beautiful pale blond aliens that looked like David Bowie and Catherine Deneuve. I hoped a spaceship would come for me and take me away from The Wolf, away from his hands and fat.

Mama says I'm anorexic because of The Wolf. Because the last time I saw The Wolf (I was sixteen) he said I was fat.

The last time, he didn't touch my breasts or thighs or ask to see me naked or to urinate in front of him. He didn't even flirt with me. I think he wasn't attracted to me anymore. This should've made me happy. Right?

But it didn't. I stopped eating.

The Wolf also said he liked me better when I was younger. This made me wonder if he was a pedophile.

When we got home to Alberta, I noticed Mama had packed one of The Wolf's shirts. She said that The Wolf wanted me to have it. It was blue. I liked the way it felt. It was probably comfortable, but I didn't dare try it on. Wearing this shirt would be like wearing him.

After I left Blueland, The Wolf played cards with other children. He only played chess with me. I wonder what he wanted from those children. Were they replacements for me who was a replacement for his daughter? A part of me was almost jealous.

These children are grown up now. I wish I could ask them if The Wolf did anything to them. If he had asked them to pee in front of him or to use the outhouse, I would be relieved. I would know for sure, I would be 100% certain, The Wolf was a wolf. I wouldn't have to feel guilty anymore.

Mama won't tell her cousins what The Wolf did. That he was bad bad bad.

When we go to Blueland, and Mama's cousins ask why I'm not going to the cemetery, Mama will say I don't like cemeteries.

But maybe I will go. Maybe to see his grave and know without a shadow of a doubt that he is dead dead dead. That it wasn't a dream or a hallucination.

When they cry tears of sorrow, I will cry tears of happiness.

Papa didn't say he wanted to kill The Wolf. He just said The Wolf was a very sick man. This isn't enough for me.

When I ask Mama if my sisters believe me, if they're on my side, Mama says they don't mention him. This isn't enough either. I want them to hate him. I would hate him if he had done it to them.

One day, I found a picture of The Wolf framed and on display on the mantel over my sister's fireplace. I was livid. I cursed her and spat on her and said I would never talk to her again, never have anything to do with her ever again. How could she put a picture of The Wolf there for everyone to see? I felt betrayed. I blamed Mama.

Mama said my sister's husband had put the picture there. That it wasn't my sister's fault. "What could she do?" Mama asked. She couldn't explain to her husband, tell him our family secrets. He mustn't know the truth. He'll think we're bad people. That we're all sick and perverted and crazy.

I blew up. I threw things. I yelled all day. I thought I was going to kill myself or Mama or both of us.

But the next day, I wasn't angry anymore. Mama said my sister put away the picture. But I didn't care anymore. I was half dead. I finally understood what had happened to The Wolf's wife. Why she was the way she was.

The Wolf's wife was a ghost of a woman. She cooked and cleaned and served her husband, but the entire time, she was half dead or numb or something. Like a zombie. Maybe something had frozen inside her when she lost her little daughter.

She never said I reminded her of her daughter. Only The Wolf said this. His wife didn't buy me things; candy, chocolate, orange pop. She did let me eat the pulp of a watermelon while she ate the part closest to the rind.

Maybe The Wolf had a mistress because his wife was almost dead, because he couldn't bear to sleep with a dead woman.

The Wolf had a gun. He let me fire it. He slept with it under his pillow. He joked that the barrel faced his wife. I thought this was funny.

I truly believed his wife would die before him. After all, she already had one foot in the grave. When The Wolf died, I was shocked. We all were.

After he died, his wife became a new woman. She came to life. She was no longer half dead, but she was insane. Completely insane.

I thought I would become just like her, because when The Wolf died, I too seemed to return to life.

CHAPTER 3

There are spaces in me like cuts scissors make. Spaces X left.

I dare not mention her name. It hurts too much. And no name suits her. Not even her own. X seems the most appropriate. In math X is unknown.

How do you write a chapter about someone you barely remember?

I can't remember her smell, the texture of her hair, the taste of her skin. All of this is lost. I have lost so much.

Her face is a shifting one. The eyes, nose, and lips change every time. My mind is always changing them.

There is very little that I remember. Almost nothing. Dr. Hill says the ECT (Electro-Convulsive Therapy) might have caused some memory loss.

Trying to remember is like waking up with a bump on the head: everything fuzzy and strange, not being able to make sense of where you are and how you got there.

Mama says it's for the better. Mama says I should never think or speak about X.

This is true love: when you can't remember. When there is a void. Not those people with their hundred stories. They are the lucky ones. They can rationalize their love. Their love has a shape.

My love is like water.

I remember X was very beautiful. Mama didn't think so, but everyone else did.

Maybe it was her beauty that drove me crazy, that pushed my mind over its threshold. Maybe I drowned in her beauty.

X's beauty was harsh. So harsh that she seemed ugly at first. Like someone from another planet, another being. She was something in between a boy and a girl. Maybe a fish like me.

It was my idea to dye her hair blonde. She'll say it was hers, but it was mine.

With blonde hair, she looked like David Bowie. David Bowie was my number one fantasy lover.

X was crazy about her age. Always lying to people that she was twenty-five. Always asking me if she was too old for me.

She had all these creams and moisturizers in her medicine cabinet. She did have a lot of wrinkles for a thirty year old woman. Probably because she drank a lot.

X fantasized about being a stripper, but when we made love for the first time, she asked me if she could keep her shirt on. I couldn't understand why. She had beautiful breasts.

X was such a mystery to me. I liked playing detective.

X always bought second hand clothes, and liked needles. These things I remember; little things that mean nothing. These are all I have to put in my pocket.

I never knew anyone who liked needles. Did she truly like needles or was she just trying to sound interesting and original? Like when she said her favourite colour was orange. Whose favourite colour is orange?

When I met X, she assumed that I wanted to be a filmmaker because I had a video camera. So, she asked me to shoot a dance she had choreographed.

Her dance partner was pretty. She looked like she could be her sister, but I knew they were lovers.

X danced with a fish. When she gutted it and smeared its guts on her chest, I fell in love with her.

I told her that I was a fish. That Mama and I were the same person. I explained but she didn't understand. She couldn't see the cord. Only Mama and I saw.

"You're crazy," X said.

X thought she was manic-depressive like me. She thought this was our attraction. She had read in a book that a lot of manic-depressives marry other manic-depressives.

But when I told her I wanted to marry her, she laughed.

When I was in the fifth grade, I had really short hair. I looked like a boy and was often mistaken for one, even though I had earrings on both ears. This confusion over my gender caused me a fair bit of anguish.

I didn't wear skirts or dresses, and being athletic didn't help.

One day, my friend Anita kissed me. It was a soft kiss on the lips. Not with tongue the way The Wolf kissed me.

Anita was pretty. Too pretty. She wore skirts and dresses. She was a different kind of girl than me.

When she gazed into my eyes, I thought she was being silly. I bonked her on the head and called her a dummy.

We were always together. We didn't play much with anyone else. The kids at school called us "lezzzies". My sisters didn't know this because they were in Junior High. And when I came home crying, I just told Mama I was going to grow my hair long.

I stopped being friends with Anita. I know this hurt her. That she was lonely and missed me. I missed her too. But I couldn't bear being called a "lezzzie".

And if ignoring Anita wasn't enough, I made sure everyone knew I jerked off two boys who were in my class that year. After that the kids stopped calling me a "lezzzie" and started calling me a "ho".

Poor Anita's heart was broken. I had broken it.

It took two years to grow my hair long. I started wearing make-up. And skirts and dresses. Mama said I looked pretty. But I always thought Mama was the pretty one.

Anita eventually moved to the west coast with her parents. She wrote me a letter, but I never wrote back.

I think loving Anita made a space in me for X. Maybe if there had been no Anita, there would be no X.

I think everyone was attracted to X. I think everyone wanted to sleep with her. And I think X wanted to sleep with everyone who wanted to sleep with her.

Maybe that's why she wanted to sleep with me.

These spaces in me make me wonder about things like this.

This is what happens when you love someone so much and you go crazy because of this love.

I could go to the restaurant and see her face so that it would no longer shift but be still. I could find peace in this stillness.

But I won't go. Oh, no.

I remember an argument we had about a prostitute. I said she was disgusting in her tight, smutty clothes.

X told me I was wrong to call her a slut, that it was sad she had to sell her body on the street, that I was the one who was disgusting because I lacked compassion.

I never called a prostitute a slut ever again.

We had a song. Or perhaps I had a song.

X laughed at me because of this song, because of my sentimentality.

A man sings it. The words are really sad. When I hear this song on the radio, it still gets under my skin.

When this song isn't playing on the radio, it's playing in my head. This song will stay with me forever. There is no escaping it. It has become a part of me. Like an arm.

I wonder if X thinks of me when she hears this song. Does she know this is the song, our song, my song, whatever?

Has she forgotten too? Was the love so great, she forgot too?

Are there spaces in X like there are spaces in me?

I wonder if she refers to me as "Amelia" or an initial or just "her". Maybe I'm "the crazy girl from eight years ago".

Does she remember my face? How sometimes my gums show when I smile?

Mama said I'd get over her. But I'm not the kind of girl who gets over things. I'm my Mama's daughter.

X lived in her grandmother's basement.

We almost burnt down the house. We were boiling spaghetti at three o'clock in the morning and had fallen asleep after a long night of lovemaking.

When the seventy year old woman made her way through the smoke and into the bedroom, she discovered me lying naked in bed with her granddaughter.

X lied to her grandmother that I was having trouble at home and had nowhere to stay. X is a great liar. She bought it.

Not only is X a liar, she is a thief too. She used to shoplift. Now, she steals money from the cash register at work. She even steals peanuts. Peanuts for Christ's sake!

I don't think that X has any guilt. The only thing she's sorry about is not getting away with more. As most criminals are.

X wanted us to rob a ski resort. She used to work at one as a waitress. I don't see how this makes her an expert.

Anyway, she had it all planned out. She said that all I had to do was hold the gun and knock the clerk unconscious.

X and I were always breaking up and making up. During one of our breakups, which lasted two weeks, X gained ten pounds. To a beautiful dancer, this is death.

X blamed me. She said I had done it to her. That it was my fault she was fat. I just laughed.

Before the weight gain, X could get away without wearing a bra. But now her perky breasts were obvious under her cotton t-shirt.

I thought she looked sexy. I made love to her that day. I stayed down there, you know where, for an hour.

When we weren't fighting, we made love every day, every possible free moment.

Once, we made love an entire weekend. We only stopped to eat food or drink beer or to go to the bathroom.

X and I were like Amazons. Like two Wonder Women.

X said she didn't like kids.

When I met her sister, to whom I wasn't attracted at all, she told me X wanted to be a mother.

I knew I had limitations, dear reader. I couldn't impregnate X. And I wasn't going to risk getting pregnant. To have a miscarriage, or a deformed child, or a mentally ill child.

I wasn't going to explain this to her sister. So I said that X was already a mother, that I was her child.

Later, X told me to do a Tarot card reading for her sister.

I was convinced that I was psychic, but X's sister could see right through me. She knew I was nuts.

X and I shared a male lover on one occasion. X wanted to see what a ménage à trois was like. I was her guinea pig.

He was a pretty boy, around my age. It should have been erotic, but it wasn't. It was nauseating. I almost threw up.

His you-know-what was so big, he had trouble entering me. It was painful. When I protested, the frustrated boy penetrated X.

When he was inside her, she was kissing me. Her moans were not for me. I yelled at her to get off me.

Later, he asked me, not X, for my phone number. I didn't give it to him. I hated him. I wanted to die. X had betrayed me in my presence.

I told X I was going to kill myself. After that, we never talked about the possibility of another threesome.

One day, I got a phone call from X's boss. She said X hadn't shown up for work.

I was worried sick. What if X was raped or killed?

I went over to her Grandma's and waited for three hours. Her Grandma didn't even offer me tea.

Later, X told me she was doing cocaine and fucking the dancer whore and the dancer whore's ugly boyfriend.

Before I overdosed on lithium, I left a message on X's Grandma's answering machine: "You disgust me."

When X visited me in the hospital, she said I ruined her life and that she was going to be alone forever.

A week later, I took her back. I thought it was all my fault, because "our" ménage à trois turned out so bad.

I was always watching X. Watching who she was watching. Watching who was watching her. Like a policeman.

I lived in fear X would cheat on me, which she did. With loads of men and women. She said she wanted to make love to everyone. Why did she need all those lovers, when all I needed was her?

Her infidelity was too much for me. I didn't know what to do. So I took on lovers too.

It became a game. She cheated on me and I cheated on her. By now I was getting good at games.

I would tell her about my conquests, torture her with details. She would torture me with secrecy.

I could have left her. She could have left me. Instead, we stuck it out like an old married couple too used to each other's ways to part.

It disgusted me to whore myself this way. I didn't have to do these things. I could have just lied. She wouldn't have known. But I did everything.

One day, I asked X, "What have I done?"

She answered, "You exist."

When X and I quarreled, I couldn't eat or sleep. This upset Mama.

Eventually, X drove me away from Mama. I moved into my own apartment. Mainly, so we could make love more often.

X didn't realize that when she was making love to me, she was making love to Mama. When she slapped me, she was slapping Mama.

I think X liked slapping me. I think it turned her on.

I didn't tell Mama X slapped me, slapped us. What would Mama think of me? That I'd let someone do that to me, to us.

Slapping turned into beatings. One day, X almost killed me. I couldn't tell Mama. I couldn't even look at her. Amelia was blue. Black and blue.

X wanted us to get a cat. She wanted to name it "Pussy".

"What else would a lesbian name her cat?" Buddy said.

The problem was that I was allergic to cats, but I was willing to take allergy pills. What were a few more pills?

I missed Mama terribly. I started smoking cigarettes. The dark circles under my eyes grew even darker. X had poisoned me with her love. I was consumed. I was dying.

The living arrangement, me paying the rent and X sponging off me, lasted less than six months.

She abandoned me like her father had abandoned her as a child. I guess the best way to get over abandonment issues is to do it to someone else.

When X left, I suffered another nervous breakdown. I was hospitalized for three months. I asked Mama every day if X had called. She never had.

Mama cursed X. She said X had almost killed her child.

When I got out of the hospital, I went home with Mama and Papa. It took them two years to nurse me back to health. I recovered, but, like Mama after Manuel's death, I would never be the same again. I was damaged.

X said when she dies she doesn't want to leave anything behind. No evidence. No trace of her existence. Nothing.

If she found out she had a terminal illness, she would burn everything: her clothes, her documents, her photographs.

Before she left me, she made me return all the photographs of her she ever gave me. Especially the naked ones.

I could have protested, but I was too weak. I gave in to her demands. I should've posted the photographs on the internet.

Maybe X hates me because I write about her, because I've immortalized her.

People ask me when I will stop writing about her. I don't know. Maybe never.

I write about her because I have nothing. Not her face, not her kiss, not her embrace.

Nothing can fill these spaces in me; no new love affair, no new infatuation, obsession, or drug.

I don't entertain the notion of ever speaking to X.

I know which restaurant she works at. I could go to that restaurant, but I don't.

Sometimes I pretend she is dead. That she never existed. This fantasy doesn't last long.

Usually, I think about X every day. Maybe five times a day. Is this a lot?

I think John Hinckley thought about Jodie Foster something like two hundred times a day.

All right, so I'm fixated. But I'm not ready to shoot a president or prime minister yet.

When I am not dreaming about the tall men I am dreaming about X.

I walk away from her. I never speak. Like the actress in that Ingmar Berman film, *Persona*.

What can I say? "I'm sorry I was ill"? "I'm sorry I was crazy"? "I'm sorry I loved you too much"?

Yes, X and I are like the actress and the nurse in the Ingmar Bergman film where they switch personalities.

Maybe I've become X. Become X, while still being Mama.

Maybe I'm a fish, Mama, Amelia Blue, The Fisherman, and X all at the same time. Yet I am nothing.

I used to watch X sleep. Sometimes I fondled her as she slept.

When she awoke, I would ask her who she was dreaming about. The clever girl said she was dreaming about me, but who knows who it could've been? Maybe her boss. Maybe her neighbour. Maybe another dancer with a dancer's body.

Sometimes, I wondered how I could exist in X's world.

What did X see in me? Me, with my ugly legs and fat ankles.

I used to play the piano quite well. I studied for several years. I was great at making stuff up. I could sit at the piano for an hour and just make stuff up. People thought I was a virtuoso.

X said she was jealous of my piano. Worried that I loved the piano more than her. She said she didn't know how she could compete with a piano.

After our grand love affair ended, and now only exists through me writing about X and X reading it, I stopped playing, couldn't play.

The breakup was as intense as a car crash. Like the one that took poor Manuel's life. It killed something in me.

It's been eight years. I haven't played for eight years. I even sold it, the piano. It was lonely and I felt it needed someone to play it.

It was a sad departure. I caressed it and said my goodbyes. I knew it was for the better.

The other day, Buddy asked me what happened to the piano. I said, "X left."

Some people have hundreds of stories. I have a handful.

I look at other women, check them out, but they do nothing for me.

I compare all women to X. All except for Mama. Mama is perfect just the way she is.

I don't want to kiss other women, fondle them, taste them. It would be strange.

I don't think I can ever love another woman. X is my one woman, my only deviation. Apart from X, I'm straight.

Maybe you think I'm disgusting. Maybe I am disgusting. But I don't think it's because I slept with a woman.

X had a polka dot ass. I kid you not. She said it was from sunburn. It must've been a pretty nasty sunburn for it to stay that way.

I know this is a very personal thing to reveal. People will know she is my X when they see her ass. But what is she going to do, sue me? Is she going to drop her drawers in front of the judge?

X liked sodomy. So did her dancer friends. I wonder if it was because of all the stretching they did.

I was not a fan of sodomy. I had never been sodomized and X was the first person I sodomized.

I did it because I loved her. In the back of my mind I always thought, "What if Mama knew?"

X and I had little contests. We'd time each other, see who could perform cunnilingus the longest. I always won.

X and I never had sex in public. X was too shy for that.

When X told her sister that she had a girlfriend, her sister was jealous. They had talked about how erotic it would be to have sex with another woman.

I thought this was a pretty weird conversation to have with your sister.

She made me buy a vibrator because her sister recommended it, but we only used it once.

I spanked X a little, tied and blindfolded her a couple of times, licked some blueberry jello off of her. Once when we were making love on my kitchen floor, X asked me to urinate on her.

I said no. I loved her, but I said no. I didn't tell her why.

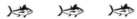

After one of our fights, X went to Vancouver to get away from me. She phoned me and made me listen to some buzzing noise. When she asked me to guess what it was, I said, "A vibrator." I was wrong. It was an electric shaver.

X made me listen to her sister shave off all the hair on her head. She went from David Bowie to Sinead O'Connor.

I guess she did it to piss me off, but it didn't matter. I loved her, with or without hair.

X's Mama is not unlike my own.

X said she clung to her Mama too. It was years before she spoke. The doctors thought she was autistic.

Perhaps I listened to X's stories and stole them. Maybe I stole X's Mama. Stole X's life. Like I stole her fish tattoo.

Maybe I did this out of revenge. Out of boredom. Because I was crazy.

Maybe I'm not even Amelia. Maybe X is Amelia. Maybe X is the manic-depressive, the fish, the one The Wolf destroyed.

Maybe I have been X all along. And you wouldn't have known if I hadn't told you.

You can't believe everything I say. Maybe my truths are only half truths. Or perhaps nothing at all.

This is what happens when you go crazy, when a crazy person goes crazy from love.

What is truth anyway? Whose truth? Maybe my truth is like my love. Without shape. Like water.

Maybe I liked X's stories and made them my own. Maybe because I was nothing and wanted to be something.

Maybe X wrote this book. And I stole her manuscript and passed it off as my own. Maybe X was the prodigy, the genius.

Maybe this is what happened: maybe I was an ordinary girl desperate to be different and interesting, so I became X.

Maybe Mama and I aren't the same person. Maybe I don't have a Mama. Maybe because I don't have a Mama, I stole X's Mama.

Maybe I'm not even crazy. Maybe I'd just rather be crazy than boring.

Who is Amelia? Who is X? Who is Mama? What does it matter? These are the ramblings of a crazy woman.

Maybe I don't even care about you, my dear reader. Maybe there are thousands of copies of this book for one sole purpose: for X to read it.

Why not just send it to her in the mail?

Because X and I, yes, me and you my darling, are still playing our little game. Only our game is not so little anymore.

We included a few people in our game before. Our friends and our lovers. Now, it's on a much grander scale. Now our game includes everyone who reads this book.

Calling you and declaring my love would be ridiculous. Or seeing you at the restaurant; anyone can do that.

No, this has to be big. I have to have my words published and available for consumption in every bookstore in the country. Maybe the world. Perhaps long after our deaths. Perhaps for eternity.

Your part in the game is to purchase this book, pay for it. This makes you a willing participant.

This is what your love has driven me to do. This is my gift to you. For all the missed birthdays and anniversaries.

How can anyone bedding you compete with this?

For my birthday, X bought me a kaleidoscope. Not one of those cheap plastic kinds. I mean one of those handmade glass ones.

After I got out of the hospital, I smashed it. This was therapeutic.

I found an old Barbie doll and cut her hair short so she would look like X. I took off her clothes and carried this naked doll with me everywhere I went. I even slept with it.

Sometimes I sodomized it. This was also therapeutic.

If I were a man, I'd have gone to the restaurant where X worked, gotten her drunk, and sodomize her for real. This is what goes through the mind of a crazy person.

I have accepted that X may never speak to me again. And that the chances of her wanting to sleep with me are as likely as winning a twenty million dollar lottery.

If X touched me now, after all these years, eight years, it would be electric. Like being struck by a bolt of lightning.

If she made love to me, it would kill me. My soul would be so elated it would rise up out of my body and float to heaven.

This is the power X has over me.

The dancer whore wasn't the only woman. There was a fat chick, too. And I don't mean fat like me. I mean really fat.

All that time I was worried about skinny dancer whores. It never occurred to me X would cheat on me with someone fatter than me.

X said it didn't count because she didn't have an orgasm. Have you heard that one before, dear reader?

I've heard X has a boyfriend now. A short boyfriend with a receding hairline. Maybe he has a big dick. She probably lets him sodomize her.

Imagining X making love with someone is agony.

X and I fit like Lego. Any other combination is obscene.

A couple of years ago, X did a dance wearing a wedding dress. This is a woman who vows she will never get married.

I didn't see her dance. I couldn't. It would've hurt too much.

I cut a picture out of a newspaper. Her head flung back. No face to correct the shifting one in my memory.

Someone else would not be able to know it's her, but I'd recognize those long skinny arms anywhere: those arms that held me, her child.

I don't remember the face. I remember her body. If I were called upon to identify X's corpse, I would know it when I saw it. I could be an expert witness.

Dear reader, I wasn't the love of X's life, if she ever loved me at all. It was a man, a painter. They were together for eight years.

X always talked about him, always compared me to him. You did this just like him, you said this just like him, you and him are the same, you'll leave me just like him.

X was obsessed with him. Like I would become with her.

I started to think about him, the painter. Formed a plan to seduce him. I would seek him out, bewitch him, and sleep with him. He lived in Europe. But I was crazy. I was willing to go to Europe. I had air miles.

During a fight, I lost my temper and revealed my plan. X wasn't even upset. She found it humorous. She said I wasn't his type, that he liked blondes.

This and the affair X had with the blonde dancer who could pass for her sister threw me into a frantic fit in which I poured a bottle of peroxide over my black Chinese hair. It stung like a hive of bees but I gritted my teeth and bore it.

My hair didn't look good. It didn't complement my olive skin. To drive me crazy, X told me she preferred brunettes. I could've strangled her and gone to prison. Because I had dyed my hair blonde and it didn't look good and I went crazy.

I remember things we did in bed, but I don't remember how it felt. This makes me very sad. X was the love of my life and I can't remember what it was like to make love to her.

X said she was raped when she lost her virginity. I began to wonder if we had too much in common: our craziness, our obsession with our weight, and our sexual abuse. Maybe I should've picked someone less damaged.

Buddy told me he thought X was a total lesbian. When I said I wouldn't be caught dead with a lesbian, he said I was homophobic. But how could I be homophobic if I was sleeping with a woman?

I'll be honest with you, dear reader, there were times when X said maybe we should just be friends. But I couldn't go backwards. I loved her. And damn it, I lusted after her. But it bothered me that I wanted a woman so much sexually.

I felt like a man always initiating the sex and being on top. This turned me on and disturbed me at the same time.

I wanted to make love with X every day, all the time. When X would shower, I'd join her. I'd start kissing and touching her and she'd complain, "I can't even take a shower without you wanting to fuck me!"

When I asked her to move in with me, she said no because she didn't think we'd get anything done. But there wasn't much to do. X was a waitress and I was living off my parents' money. When X quit her job, we watched TV all day.

At one point, X said she never wanted to have sex ever again. This lasted about a week, but it wasn't me she ended her celibacy with.

One day, I was taking a bath with X. She was kissing and touching me. I was very turned on. Then, she told me she was a lesbian.

I thought X and I were both heterosexual women with the exception of being attracted to one woman. I was all right with this, but I wasn't all right with X being attracted to more than one woman, more than me.

When I got out of the tub, X said she was joking.

I don't know if she was joking or not. You never could tell with X. It reminded me of when someone tells you you got a bad haircut and they see they've hurt your feelings so they say "Just kidding." You know these people.

X had some scary stories, like the one where her painter boyfriend raped her and to get revenge she bit his dick.

After that, I was always a little uneasy when she was doing you-know-what to me.

X never said that I was too fat, but she did complain about me shaving off all my pubic hair.

She begged me to grow it back. When I said no, she asked me if she could shave it for me. Dear reader, would you trust X with a razor?

After our last serious fight, I was so desperate to get her back, I said I'd let her shave my pussy or I'd grow it back, whatever she wanted, but she wouldn't take me back.

X told me that she had to get a restraining order against one of her lovers. I wondered if this was a pattern with X, that when people fall in love with her they become obsessed and go crazy. Was there something about X that fucked people up?

Oh well. At least I wasn't the only one.

I walk by the restaurant. X's back is facing me. I notice her long skinny arms. I know I'm not crazy any more. Mama and Papa and Dr. Hill say I'm not crazy. What if I still am? What if X turns around and sees the craziness in my eyes?

I cross the street and postpone looking at X for another day. Maybe another year; maybe another life.

I go home and write.

CHAPTER 4

Francis

My lover is a hemophiliac with yellow irises. Two suns burning into me.

My lover is an orphan. I offer him my heart, my home, my family. Yet, he's lonely.

My lover is a poet. His words are tentacles, and because I'm a poet too, I can't pull away.

My friends think Francis is plain, yet his beauty engulfs me.

When he weeps, I crush him in my arms.

Francis likes to bleed. He has scars on his arms and legs.

He says he does it because his real Mama abandoned him, but he's usually bloody after we quarrel.

Every day, I search his body for fresh cuts. I scold him. Secretly, I'm a vampire.

Francis has written seven poems about me. I've written forty-three about him. My Mama's Papa's Mama told me that one person always loves the other more.

Thoughts of Francis exhaust me. Thoughts of hair, skin, and mouth. I would die for him. He says he'd die for me too, but I think he's just suicidal.

Francis spends his money on CDs and martinis. I spend my money on Francis. My parents think he's a parasite. I love him anyway.

Francis says if he had to choose between me and his Tori Amos CDs, he'd pick the CDs.

I ask Dr. Hill if he thinks Francis loves me. He says he does. If Dr. Hill thinks so, it must be true.

I ask Buddy too. Buddy says, "Yes, he loves you…in his own sick way."

Francis was a very sick baby. His real Mama left him in the hospital and never came back. Almost a year later, he was adopted.

Francis had fuzzy black hair. His adoptive parents told him he was an Eskimo. This can't be true. My editor says Eskimos don't carry the hemophilia gene.

Francis is always telling people horror stories about his adoptive family. He even wrote a letter to Oprah.

Francis claims his three hundred pound adoptive Mama beat him and his schizophrenic adoptive older sister molested him.

Deep down, I don't believe Francis was abused. I almost don't believe he was adopted.

I'm supposed to feel sorry for Francis. I'm supposed to say, "Poor, poor Francis."

He doesn't want to talk about what happened to me. There's room for only one victim in this relationship.

I never cry in front of Francis. He doesn't want to be around me when I'm depressed. He won't let me be my manic-depressive self. And that is exhausting. Smile smile rest. Smile smile rest. Smile smile sleep.

Francis gives me so many headaches, I'm going to overdose on aspirin.

Most of the time, I want to inflict horrible pain on Francis.

Sometimes, I want to kill him, slice him open, disembowel him, eat his heart, and drink his blood.

Dr. Hill reassures me that I'm not a psychopath. He says I'm not neat enough to be one. He advises me to stay away from Francis. Stay far far away.

Dr. Hill says if I get a criminal record, I might not be able to leave the country.

"You want to go to New Orleans for Mardi Gras, don't you?" he reminds me. I nod my head.

Francis wants to find his real Mama. Maybe she would love him.

A private investigator told Francis it would cost thousands of dollars to find her. So I bought Francis a big piggy bank. I put a dollar in it every time we made love.

Francis's younger adoptive sister is a lesbian. I've never met her, never even seen a picture of her.

I was always asking Francis about his sister. I just wanted to understand lesbians better. Maybe Francis was worried I'd be attracted to her, that I'd fall in love with her.

Sometimes, Francis goes to the gay bar with his sister. He never asks me to come. When I ask him if men ever hit on him, he says no.

What if Buddy is right? What if Francis is gay? What if he's leading a double life, one with me, and the other at the gay bar?

Francis told me he had slept with a man once.

I asked Francis: Was he feminine? Was he a top or a bottom? Did he have a big penis?

Francis just said he was an ordinary guy.

After this confession, I watched Francis closely whenever we were out in public, to check if he was checking out any men, whether it was the theatre usher, the waiter, the bartender, the coat check boy. I was checking if Francis was checking out the coat check boy.

Francis reassures me that he's straight. I'm worried he'll end up like Buddy. Like Mama always says, "Once is enough."

Francis wrote his family a letter. In it he explained what his older sister did to him and how unhappy he was growing up, that he no longer wanted to be part of the family.

Francis's Mama was very upset by this letter. I told Francis he did the right thing, but the truth was, I just wanted Francis to stop talking about it. I liked it better when he was using his mouth for something else.

Despite the letter, Francis spent Christmas with his family. He got everyone presents except for his Mama and his older sister, but he still talked to them.

Later, he cried in my arms. He said he wished he were dead. I kissed him over and over. I fell in love with him again.

Sometimes, I think about cutting myself, but I'm too squeamish. I can barely put up with having a needle in my arm every two weeks.

I don't think badly of Francis because he cuts himself. Some people cut themselves. Some people want you to urinate on them.

However, I did worry about Francis. After all, he was a hemophiliac. What if he bled to death?

I suppose being a hemophiliac made it more fun. There was an element of danger.

Francis shows me his bruises like a proud hemophiliac. He hides his cuts but shows off his bruises. Go figure.

Francis is so…well, so *Francis*.

Maybe I love him because I want to be doomed, want to die. Francis is my exit. The noose around my neck.

I would never have his baby. He would be jealous of his own baby. He would drink all of my milk.

Francis is always hungry, always thirsty, always wanting more. I'm like Ethiopia, dry and starving.

At night, I wrap my hands around Francis's throat as he sleeps. I have to fight the urge to choke him.

I want him to stop. Stop being so Francis.

Francis has ugly toenails. Not the ugliest I've seen, but pretty ugly. When I told him he should get a pedicure, he cut himself.

Shit, he can't take any criticism. Maybe I should've criticized him all day until he was covered in cuts from head to toe and bled to death.

I am so aware of Francis's misery, I've neglected my own.

When Francis tells me of his abuse, of his despair, I want to give him an orgasm.

Francis with his black heart and his ugly toenails is the object of my affection. He is the only lover I don't pretend is X. When I'm making love to Francis, I'm making love to Francis.

Buddy thinks Francis is as deep as a puddle. But he's wrong. Francis is a river.

I love Francis. I do, but not like X. X is in my roots. You can cut the tree, but unless you pull out the roots, it'll just keep growing

Francis has no talent. He is talentless. Apart from having some potential as a writer, he can't sing or dance or so much as play a recorder. He can't even play "Three Blind Mice" or "Hot Cross Buns" on a fucking recorder. He is hopeless.

Francis envies me because I've been published. I envy Francis too.

I write because I can. Francis writes because it's his passion. Writing is everything to Francis. He is nothing without his writing. It's his core, his centre.

He writes all day. Every day. And when he's not writing, he's thinking or talking about writing. I'm in awe of Francis. He's what a real writer is supposed to be. I wish what exists inside him existed inside me.

When Francis asked me to read his poetry, I told him it was shit. The next day, he had ten cuts and his fingernails were half eaten. I kissed every cut and finger and whispered "chrysanthemum". Francis whispered back "tarantula".

I tried to help Francis become a better writer.

When I criticized him, I did this out of love.

I helped Francis put together a manuscript. I even wrote a letter of recommendation. I submitted this to my publishers.

When Francis received the rejection letter, he threatened to kill himself.

He was jealous. I was published and he was not. This made me the enemy.

Maybe I did get his hopes up, but I was just trying to be a good girlfriend. I didn't say he was going to get published for sure.

It's a tough profession. Most writers aren't happy people. They struggle, they suffer. A lot of writers are poor. Some of them kill themselves.

Francis dreamed of the day his name and picture were going to be on a book. When he told me this, I thought he was pathetic, but his tears moved me. He made me feel ashamed of being a writer, of not liking writing more.

Francis would cry and say, ""I just want to be a writer," and I would stroke his hair and say, "You will be. You will be."

Afterwards, Francis started lying to people that my publishers were going to publish him.

When Francis told me his adoptive sister made him perform cunnilingus on her, I crumbled and forgave him.

I begged Francis to tell me more about his perverted older sister and his tyrannical Mama. I liked hearing Francis' sad stories, especially before making love. This was foreplay for me.

Francis shouldn't compare himself to me. I'm several years older. Besides, I was a child prodigy and I'm manic-depressive. Maybe this is the formula for a writer.

Feeling depressed all the time and wanting to kill yourself isn't very romantic. Francis shouldn't want to be like me. I don't.

Sometimes, Francis thinks he's manic-depressive too. I just think he's fucked.

Francis says he'd be so happy if he got published. That's what I thought.

Maybe the problem is that Francis wants it too much. I mean, look at me. I don't want to be a writer. Maybe anyone who really enjoys writing shouldn't be a writer. If it doesn't hurt, if you don't suffer, something is wrong.

I asked Dr. Hill to help Francis.

Francis went a few times. He gave up when Dr. Hill suggested that Francis try medication. Francis was opposed to this because it meant he would have to stop drinking.

"Fuck pills," he said. Yet, he was perfectly all right with taking Ecstacy.

I hate it when Francis is happy. I want him to be miserable all the time. I like him best when he's miserable.

Francis is always trying to be funny in front of me.

I tell him he doesn't have to be funny. Buddy is funny, and that's enough for me.

Besides, I'm not attracted to funny. Melancholy and tragic turn me on.

Francis is obsessed with the singer Tori Amos. He e-mails other Tori fans he meets on the internet. He tells these people about our problems. I think this is crazy.

Yeah, Tori is wonderful. But Francis's dream is to be a writer, not a singer. I'm a fucking writer, a real fucking writer, a fucking published writer. He should be my fan. He should idolize me. Don't you think so, dear reader?

Maybe I should dye my hair red like Tori, and start playing the piano again.

Maybe Francis would've loved me more had he met me before X broke my heart and I sold my piano.

I wonder who's playing my piano now.

Francis had two roommates, both girls, like in *Three's Company*. One worked during the day and the other at night, so one was always home. Francis didn't even have a room. He slept on the couch. We definitely couldn't have sex at his place.

As for me, I was too ashamed to bring him home to my parents.

If we had a car, we could drive to the woods. Only I stopped driving when Manuel died. Francis didn't even have a driver's license.

We decided to go to a hotel. I paid.

Later, one of his roommates moved out and Francis got his own room. He told me not to moan so loud when I was having an orgasm. He worried that the people downstairs would hear. "Fuck you," I said.

Francis eventually wanted us to move into an apartment together, but I wasn't going to leave Mama for stupid Francis.

I've never seen Francis eat. I'm fatter than him. It bothers me that I'm fatter. Mama says the man should always be fatter than the woman.

The first time Francis saw me naked, I asked if I have an ugly body. His response was, "No body is ugly." What kind of fucking answer is that?

I cried when we made love. I told him I missed X, that I loved X so much I was going to die.

Francis was very hurt by this. I read about it in his diary.

I guess when you sleep with someone for the first time, they don't want to hear that you'd rather be with someone else. I guess this is a no no.

Francis is the complete opposite of X. I had to drag information out of X. Francis is an open book. He will tell you anything. Now, I almost respect X for being so secretive.

X is shy and introverted. Francis needs lots and lots of attention. He's like a kid. Sometimes, I felt like I was his Mama.

X is an intellectual. She reads at least half an hour a day about things like psychology and art.

I never saw Francis even pick up a book. I think mine was the first one he had read since high school.

I told him if he wanted to be a writer that he should read more. I said this to help him. He thought I was being a bitch. Maybe I was a little.

It bothered Francis that I always wrote about X. "It's been four years," he'd say. I told Francis not to worry, that I'd write about him too someday.

Francis thinks four years is plenty of time to get over someone, that it's not normal to still have a broken heart.

We all have our vices. Some people smoke. Francis cuts himself. I'm obsessed with X.

Francis couldn't understand why I was so obsessed with X. "No more X!" he would yell, and then "Why can't you say her name? She does have a name?"

Francis thought X was okay looking. That she had a nice smile. He didn't think she was the kind of girl you get obsessed with.

Every day, Francis had a small soup and crackers at the restaurant where X worked. He said he went because his roommate worked there. I begged Francis to stop going there, to stop talking to X.

What if Francis wanted to sleep with X? Maybe the key to the mystery was in her lovemaking.

It would sort of turn me on if Francis slept with X, but I don't think X would go for a loser like Francis.

Francis calls me twenty times a day from work. I can't believe they don't fire him. He calls to complain how bad his life is.

It is like a competition. Whose life is worse? Who is more depressed? Who wants to die more?

"At least you have a Mama," he says. "At least your Mama didn't abandon you." This is his last resort, when he has nothing else to use.

Francis calls me Dollface. I like it when he calls me that, but maybe he calls everyone that like the way some people call everyone sweetie. My sisters and Mama say sweetie all the time. It's sweetie this and sweetie that.

One day, I saw a movie where this woman called everyone Dollface. Francis must have stolen it.

Francis said he wanted to get a tattoo of a stingray. This was the first original thought Francis had. I was impressed. But a part of me wondered if he'd stolen that too.

Francis has horrible taste in movies, When we went to see a movie, it always had to be something he wanted to see. Usually, it was crap.

I'd sit in the dark bored out of my mind. This is how the fondling began, out of boredom, because Francis had horrible taste in movies.

After a while, I stopped minding for paying for our tickets, stopped minding we were seeing crappy movies. It was so exciting to touch each other in the dark, in public.

We started seeing two or three movies a week. I can't even remember what movies we saw.

I'd bring Francis close to orgasm and stop. I was cruel to him. I enjoyed being cruel to him.

I wanted to kill and kiss Francis at the same time. He aroused anger and passion in me. This can't be a healthy combination.

I fantasized about cutting Francis.

When I'd tell him he was a terrible lover, nothing compared to X, he looked destroyed.

I got so aroused when I saw him cry. He is so attractive to me when he's miserable. His sorrow is so beautiful and intense, I feel like an empty bottle being filled with water. The closer Francis is to committing suicide, the more enamoured I am with him.

There's no smiling or laughing allowed during sex. This is forbidden. I want tears. I want pain. I want suffering.

I convulsed with excitement as his depressed fingertips grazed my skin.

Francis and I would be out on a date, say having dinner. In the middle of dinner, he would excuse himself to go to the bathroom. Instead of going to the bathroom, he'd go home.

I'd wait and wait. Then, I'd check the men's bathroom. Yup, he ditched me. I felt like such a fool.

The next day, Francis would call me and say he had to go home because his stomach hurt.

When I broke up with him, he said he had cancer.

Buddy said, "Cancer shmancer. Pllllllease."

It should've been over, but I stayed with Francis.

A month later, he told me his doctor said the cancer disappeared. Poof. Just like that.

Lying to someone that you have cancer has got to be the lowest you can go.

I think Francis is cheating on me with his roommate. She's thinner than me.

I still date other men, and Francis knows it. I make sure he knows it.

Dr. Hill says there's nothing wrong with making new friends. It's not like I am having intercourse.

I only fuck someone if Francis and I are on a break. This doesn't count.

Francis cheated on me once with his ex-girlfriend. To punish him, I fucked two guys.

If someone fucks me over once, I fuck them over twice. This is my policy. I think this is a good policy, don't you?

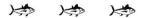

We were always fighting, so we had a lot of angry sex. Have you ever had angry sex? It's quite something.

I'd say, "Fuck me harder you fucking bastard!" and Francis would say, "I'm fucking you harder you fucking bitch!"

Sometimes, I think we fought just to have good sex. If it weren't for the sex, I would've left Francis a lot sooner.

Francis and I also had phone sex. We'd talk dirty and listen to each other masturbate. I was paranoid someone would pick up the phone or some truck driver could pick up our signal on his CB radio. I could just hear him saying, "Phone sex 10-4".

One day, Francis showed up in front of Dr. Hill's office. He told me I was a bad lover and that my cum tasted bad.

I remember him being so close to my face, an inch away from my mouth. I could've kissed him.

I did a judo leg sweep and Francis fell to the ground. I caught his head in my hand so it wouldn't hit the hard floor and crack open like a watermelon. Then, I punched his face carefully, not to break his nose. Everything was in slo-mo, like in *The Matrix*. Finally, all those years of martial arts paid off.

A month after I broke up with Francis, he showed up at the café he knows I go to with a tall skinny ugly mannish girl. They were very affectionate, holding hands. In the entire year I had been with Francis, not once did he hold my hand in public.

I was shocked and repulsed. I wished Francis had showed up with a pretty girl. Then I could be jealous.

How could he stoop so low? How could he go from me to that "it"? Not even a beautiful "it" like X, and certainly not a fish like me.

When I asked him if he had slept with it, that thing, that ugly thing, he replied, "Of course."

Of course? What did he mean of course? She's fucking disgusting! I mean yuck!

There will never be another chance for Francis. He ruined his chances by holding that thing's hand. I will never forgive him, no matter what else his older sister did to him.

Three months later, I see Francis and "it" at a movie theatre. I wonder if "it" is still his girlfriend, if they're fondling each other in the theatre.

Again, I feel repulsed. I get a better look at her this time and I think she is even uglier than the first time I saw her. What can Francis possibly see in her? She looks so manly. Is Francis gay?

Francis keeps calling and hanging up. I know it's him.

One day, he asks if I miss him. I say no. It doesn't hurt me to say no. In fact, I revel in it.

If Francis continues to harass me, I'll get a restraining order. I will revel in that too. I would love to see Francis behind bars.

I think Francis has abandonment issues like X. I think he wants me because he can't have me.

I ask Dr. Hill what kind of a person calls you after you've beaten them up in public. "A crazy person," answers Dr. Hill.

If Francis thinks this is a game, he's playing with the wrong person. I'm a fucking pro now.

When Francis calls and says he's going to kill himself, I tell him he's nothing. I tell myself he's nothing.

"He's crazy," I say to my friends. I see myself now. I am X, uttering words she uttered.

Francis can go on fucking *Oprah* and tell the world what a terrible girlfriend I was. I don't give a fuck!

If Oprah's people phone me and ask me to be a guest, to be reunited with Francis, to try to work things out, I will refuse. Even if Oprah herself calls and begs me and I get to stay at a four star hotel and eat all the deep dish Chicago pizza I want, I will say, "No. I'm sorry, Oprah, but no."

Mama and Papa worry when Francis calls. They think he's crazy. They tell me to be careful, that he might be following me. He might rape me or kidnap me or kill me. All my life I've had to worry about someone raping me, kidnapping me, or killing me.

Dear reader, sometimes I feel a little bit good when Francis calls, but Francis isn't calling because of Amelia Blue. Francis is calling because of Francis. When I realize this, I no longer feel good. This time I'm the one with the stomach ache.

It's been almost two years since I dumped Francis, but he still calls.

Sometimes, I get the feeling Francis is talking or thinking about me. It's a strange fuzzy feeling. It's hard to explain. He usually calls when I get this feeling. He calls and hangs up. I know it's him because we have call display. I think he wants me to know it's him. It's kind of creepy. No, it is creepy.

I guess, whether or not I like it, Francis and I have a connection. Maybe it's like the cord between Mama and me. Except Mama is wonderful, and Francis is not. I don't want to have a connection with a crazy loser who lies that he has cancer.

It reminds me of that story about the twins. The one in Asia feels the other one in North America burn her hand on the stove. Maybe Francis is like my twin, or maybe he was my twin in a past life. Maybe he had cancer in a past life too.

I wonder if Francis is still fucking "it".

I bet "it" tells Francis his poetry is amazing. I bet "it" performs fellatio for Francis whenever he wants. Francis probably just lies still while "it" does everything. He's so lazy.

I wonder if Francis phones "it" twenty times a day. I wonder if he calls her Dollface.

I'm always worried that I'm going to bump into "it". I ask Buddy what I should do if she provokes me. Buddy says, "You'll just have to beat her up too, Bruce."

One day, when I'm rich and famous, Francis will never be able to get a hold of me unless he writes to my fan club. They'll just think he's an obsessed psycho, which he is.

Dr. Hill thinks Francis is dangerous, that you can never overestimate a psycho. It's like in films where the police have to shoot the bad guy like fifty times before he dies. Maybe Francis will keep coming back no matter how many times I beat him up.

The last time he called, he asked me if I still loved him. Without any hesitation I said, "You disgust me" and hung up.

When I told Buddy the story, he was in complete admiration. He practiced saying, "You disgust me" in front of the mirror every day. He could hardly wait to use it on one of his lovers. He ended up using it on me.

I wonder how much longer Francis will keep on calling me. A year? Five years? Is he still going to call me when I'm a little old lady?

I should get a restraining order against Francis. If it was anyone else, I would. Dear reader, don't think I wouldn't get a restraining order on you if you crossed the line. I don't because I still love him a tiny bit. We're talking about a very tiny bit.

I'm not afraid Francis will hurt me. I'm afraid that I will hurt him.

I don't want a criminal record. I want to go to Mardi Gras.

CHAPTER 5

VINCENT

69

I step out of the shower.
I stare at my fat.
Vincent is awake.
He looks like an old man.
His eyes crawl on my flesh like spiders.
I am 8 or 12 or 14.
Vincent is The Wolf watching me dress.

I was walking down Jasper Avenue, on my way to a ménage à trois. I was just about to ask someone for directions when a handsome man in his forties asked me for directions. Weird, huh? Destiny, I thought.

This handsome man was from Chicago, the windy city.

"So how windy is it?" I asked.

"Pretty windy," he said.

"That's where Oprah lives," I said.

"That's right," he responded.

I can't remember where he wanted to go. Or where I was going. Only that we were both lost.

We were two lost souls meant to find each other. And upon finding each other, no longer be lost.

We decided to walk in the same direction, straight.

I loved his hair. It was blond and thick. Short, but lots of it. I wanted to run my fingers through it. And he had these cool spectacles. He looked really smart, like a genius or something.

I remember he was wearing shorts and a t-shirt. So it must've been summer. Yes, it was a nice summer afternoon and I was on my way to a ménage à trois when a handsome man from Chicago asked me for directions.

You probably want to know about the ménage à trois. Well, there's not much to tell. Some girl I knew asked me if I would want to sleep with her and her boyfriend and I said, "Sure, why not?" These kinds of situations come easily for me. I don't know why. They just do.

After we walked straight for a few blocks, we found the handsome Chicago man's hotel. The plan was that we were going to go to his hotel room and he was going to change clothes and he was going to take me out for dinner.

What was I doing going to this stranger's hotel room? Maybe he wasn't from Chicago. Maybe this was a line. He could've been a psycho, a rapist, a murderer. I was too depressed to care. This is why I was going to have a ménage à trois. Because I was bored and depressed.

Some girls wouldn't have gone with him to his hotel room. But I was crazy.

When we were alone in the elevator, I pressed a button to stop the elevator and I leaned over and kissed him and grabbed his you-know-what.

When we got to his room, I took my clothes off and let him fuck me. I had some condoms in my purse. Mama makes me always carry them in case someone wants to rape me. I am supposed to ask my rapist to please put one on.

I was so depressed. My pulse hardly went up.

After he came, I asked him what his name was. He said, "Vincent." I had never slept with someone who's name started with a V.

I usually don't have intercourse with strangers. I'll do other things, but I usually don't have intercourse until at least the second time I see them. Maybe it was because I was so depressed, or because of his thick blond hair, or because he could quote Shakespeare. Or maybe that summer afternoon was just a perfect day to have intercourse. Maybe it was as simple as that.

Dear reader, you must think I'm bad.

If I had never seen Vincent again, I probably would've felt guilty for having sex with him ten minutes after meeting him. But because he ended up being my boyfriend, it was alright. I wasn't a slut. It was just love at first sight.

I ask Mama if I can still live with her when I am married.

"You and your husband?" she asks.

"No, just me," I say.

"Where would he live?"

"In his own home."

Mama warned me. She said that even if I find happiness with Vincent, the depression won't go away, that I should be prepared for this.

I thought I was going to marry Vincent. When I told my sisters, they were overjoyed. They took me shopping, to see movies, to eat out. I felt like a debutante, like I had passed initiation. My sisters were saying, "Hello world! This is our newly heterosexual sister and we are so proud of her!"

Vincent is named after my favourite painter. And his favourite colour is blue.

Vincent always quotes Shakespeare. People think he's clever.

He looks like the British actor Kenneth Branagh. Except Vincent has a goatee and spectacles.

Sometimes I would pretend he was Kenneth Branagh. I even got him to fake a British accent when we had sex.

When Buddy asked me to describe him, I told Buddy his height and weight. I described him like I would describe a criminal to the police. I didn't say Vincent was charming or clever.

Sometimes when I looked at Vincent I saw an old man. In some light, his blond hair looks gray.

I wondered if I would give him a heart attack in bed. If I would kill him with my young hips and my tight vagina.

When I had alcohol, he scolded me like he was my father. This felt a little creepy.

Vincent paid for everything. Dinners, movies, hotel rooms, sex toys. He wasn't like Francis.

Vincent did a lot of traveling. He was some sort of business man like The Wolf.

He loves rollercoasters. He goes on one in each city he visits.

He thought I was with him because of the money. I liked him with the money. He was attractive to me with the money. But I was with him because of the sex.

Vincent was good to me. He did everything I asked him to. When I asked him to spank me, he did. When I asked him to rape me, he did. What more did I want? He was the closest thing to being on batteries.

When Vincent said he liked my body, my breasts, I thought he was crazy or lying. I'm not anyone's dream girl, with my fat ankles and my ugly legs. Vincent could have any girl he wanted. Why me?

Vincent said I was a good person. I think he was with me because I was good in bed. I think he was in it for the sex. He disguised it nicely, in shiny wrapping paper and a big red bow, but I knew the truth. Vincent had been on rollercoasters all over the world, but I was spectacular.

There are two things I know about myself. I am a good lover. And I can write.

If you are a book critic and you give me a bad review, I don't give a fuck because I know I got here with my brain not my pussy. So, fuck you!

My editor says a lot of sex abuse victims feel their self worth is connected to their sexuality, their attractiveness or ability as a lover.

I didn't tell Vincent about The Wolf. I didn't want to feel like a victim with Vincent. I didn't want this shit to be in the back of his mind when I ask him to hit me or rape me. My confession would ruin our sex life. And I needed this kinky sex more than anything else Vincent could offer.

I also didn't tell Vincent about how Mama and I were the same and about the invisible cord that could stretch stretch stretch. I would not be an open book like Francis.

Why should I expose myself to Vincent? Why should I give him a glimpse of my soul? I was going to wait 'til we were married, 'til I had my American citizenship, 'til we were living in L.A. Maybe even then I wouldn't tell him.

Besides, Mama says men get bored easily. A woman needs to be mysterious to keep a man's interest.

Some people have been to fucking prison and fucking killed someone and they don't tell their lover. I don't have to tell Vincent fuck all.

Receiving mail from Vincent became a ritual. Mama would go get the mail and she'd say "Guess what?" Then, Mama and I would sit down, have an espresso and I would read what Vincent wrote me. I'd skip the naughty bits.

I have a special box for Vincent's letters and postcards. I am like Mama with her treasure chest. I am in love with Vincent's words like Mama was with Papa's. Being in love with someone's words is almost like being in love with them. Close enough for me anyway.

It's so exciting when a florist calls you and asks if you will be home at a certain hour so they can deliver some flowers someone has sent you. Mama and I were so happy. Except Mama and I are never happy.

I had waited my whole life for a man like Vincent. Vincent lived in Chicago but he always sent me roses. I've gone out with a guy that lived across the street from me and he could've picked some flowers from his mother's fucking garden and walked over to my house and given them to me but he didn't.

Vincent was the first person, other than Papa, who sent me roses. Was this merely coincidence or was it fate? If you are crazy, you will think it's fate. To a crazy person there are no accidents, no coincidences. Everything is destined, meant to be. It's from people like me that the psychic hotlines make the big money.

Papa said he thought the right guy had come along. He hadn't even met Vincent. Papa had never said this about any guy. He didn't even mind the twenty year age difference.

Vincent was as close to Manuel as I was going to get. Besides, I was too lazy to wait for my real soul mate.

When I told him I couldn't have children, he didn't mind. He said we could adopt. That it would be good to give an unfortunate child a home. But I don't think they just give kids to any crazy person who wants one.

When I look back on my relationship, it feels like a marriage. Like Vincent was my husband.

Now, when people ask me if I was married, I want to say "yes". Like yes is the right answer. After all, I was married to Vincent in my heart.

Vincent and I mostly had a long distance relationship. He could've had another girlfriend or a wife. He could've had a harem. And a hundred children.

But where would he get the time to call me every night and write me all those letters and postcards and send me flowers? I mean, the guy had a job.

People say long distance relationships are hard. I think they're perfect for a manic-depressive. Distance was what I needed. If Vincent were around all the time, he'd see just how crazy I am. And he'd surely leave me. I could hide all this crap when he was in Chicago.

I didn't write Vincent any letters or postcards. It was all about me.

I came to realize that when people talk about being old fashioned in dating, it means that the man does all the work. I always prided myself on being modern, but being old fashioned was pretty good.

I got a lot more out of being in a relationship with a man than with a woman. When I was with a woman, I gave and gave. And Francis was practically a woman, so it was the same with him. With Vincent it was different. I was on the receiving end.

I thanked Vincent for being so good to me the best way I could, with sex. Maybe I should've told him I loved him or written him a poem.

Vincent phoned me every evening at 9 o'clock. I looked forward to his phone calls. It was the most exciting part of my day.

We usually talked for half an hour. I took my meds at 9:00 and they would kick in by 9:30 which is when I'd be finished talking to Vincent.

So after I talked to Vincent I would enter a deep sleep. Having spoken to Vincent made this slumber even sweeter.

Mama looked forward to these phone calls too. Mama was happy. Her daughter had a real boyfriend, a heterosexual man who was husband material. I saw Mama's happiness and I didn't want to spoil it. Poor Mama was rarely happy, mostly because of me.

What would happen if Vincent didn't call one night? Would it totally fuck me up? Would I go crazy and kill myself? Mama worried about this too.

I had grown dependent on these phone calls. I needed them. They were addictive.

One night, Vincent did not call at 9:00. The next half hour was dreadful. Every minute was painful. Mama was distraught too. When she saw the look on my face, she said, "He'll call."

At 9:30 my meds kicked in and as usual I went to bed and fell asleep.

I didn't find out that Vincent had called at 9:45 until the next morning. Mama said Vincent was deeply apologetic. That something had come up and he had to phone his sister. Maybe he was lying. Maybe he was screwing someone else. But I was happy.

I was miserable too though. Miserable because I realized how depressed I would be without Vincent. I got a taste of how I'd feel if Vincent stopped calling me.

I loved X. And Francis. And Buddy. But it was Vincent I didn't think I could live without.

I had turned into one of those women I never wanted to be.

What was going to happen to me? Was I going to marry Vincent and become a housewife?

Would I stop writing? Would I become happy and have nothing to write about? Isn't this what every creative person is afraid of? We desperately don't want to be depressed anymore, yet we cling to our depression and worry what will happen to us if we're no longer depressed.

I was working. Yes, I had a job. A stupid job, but a job. I worked in a sock store. We sold only socks and pantyhose. I had to know how much lycra there was in every pantyhose.

Everything was going fine. Then out of the blue, BOOM! I crashed. I had another nervous breakdown.

I was hospitalized Yes, manic-depressives often have nervous breakdowns and are hospitalized. The slutty manager of the sock store, who was supposed to be my friend, fired me when I was hospitalized.

When Vincent called, Mama told him the truth.

His reaction was perfect. He passed the fucking test. He didn't freak out and ditch me. He stuck with me through the worst. In sickness and in health.

He sent more flowers and letters and postcards. He wrote that he was sorry. That he hoped I would be better soon, and he "cared a lot". Mama cried when she read my letters. She said she saw Papa in Vincent.

Vincent called Mama and talked to her while I was in the hospital, which was about six weeks. Mama became very fond of Vincent.

Papa joked that Vincent was his son in law. But Papa hardly spoke to him. Papa didn't want to interfere.

When I had my breakdown, for no apparent reason except that I was manic-depressive, I stopped caring, loving Vincent. This is when I changed. This was the turning point. When I started hating him. This is what a nervous breakdown can do.

I remember feeling grouchy all the time. I was angry at everyone. Especially Vincent. The next time my sisters asked me about Vincent, I told them to fuck off. I even yelled at Mama and Papa.

When I got out of the hospital, I had gained ten pounds. That fucking food was so fattening. Do not, I repeat, do not eat their meat! Lie that you are vegetarian!

Vincent wanted to visit me, to see me as soon as possible, to meet my parents and my sisters. But I was so fat.

I don't know if the breakdown created a lot of bullshit or made me see the bullshit that was already there. I became paranoid. Always asking Vincent if he was seeing someone else, if he was cheating on me. I accused him of lying, of not caring about me, just using me for sex, only wanting me because I was so much younger.

I was damaged by the nervous breakdown. The part of me that could love was damaged. I'm sorry this happened, that my love for Vincent changed. That I changed. That everything went downhill from that point. That everything turned to shit.

It's pretty sad that this happened to me. I know you'll agree.

This was my big chance at love, and it went down the drain.

I regretted ever telling Vincent that I was depressed.

Sometimes I felt like a science experiment. If I was quiet, he'd ask me, "Are you depressed?" or "Do you need a tranquilizer?"

When I said I was depressed, he asked me, "Do you want to kill yourself?" and "How would you do it?"

It was like fucking Sigmund Freud!

Vincent says he understands me because his sister is manic-depressive.

I hate it when people think because they know one manic-depressive, they know them all.

When I said, "Stop telling me you understand," he said, "I understand."

Maybe he thought having a bipolar sister was the training wheels for having a bipolar girlfriend.

Vincent's sister is a shopoholic. Sometimes, she spends thousands of dollars in one day.

I too am a shopoholic. But I limit myself to the dollar store. Once I spent eighty dollars. That's not a lot. But that's eighty fucking items!

I ask Vincent if he's read *The Bell Jar*. He says he hasn't. I tell him he can't possibly understand manic depression until he's read Sylvia Plath's writing.

Even when he does read it, Vincent still won't understand me. I am intangible. I have no shape. Like water. Only a fish can understand me. And Vincent is no fish.

Vincent says he scored genius on an I.Q. test. I don't believe him.

If he did, it still doesn't give him a reason to think he knows more about my own illness than I do.

"You should rest."

"You should take a tranquilizer."

"You shouldn't drink."

He started telling me not to bite my nails. Not to eat too fast. To chew my food carefully.

He kept a calendar like Mama did. He would tell me when to take my meds and he monitored my mood swings.

He even wrote down when I got my periods.

He was my Mama, Papa, and Dr. Hill all rolled in one.

I wasn't going to listen to him. Not because he was twenty years older, and certainly not because he scored high on an I.Q. test.

I tell Vincent he is a thief, that Shakespeare was a thief, and so am I.

Vincent steals from Shakespeare.

Shakespeare stole from Marlowe.

I steal from Marguerite Duras.

Marlowe and Duras probably stole too.

We are all thieves.

We are all pieces of each other.

My damaged mind began to think about X again. I started to compare Vincent to X. And Vincent couldn't measure up.

I started talking about X again too. A lot. Mama couldn't understand why. I didn't know why either. Especially now that I found the perfect boyfriend who would've made the perfect husband.

I stared at the picture of X I had cut out of the newspaper. The one of her in the wedding dress. I missed those skinny arms. Where was X? Who was she with? What was she doing?

I didn't know why I was thinking about X. Except because I'd gone crazy, which was Dr. Hill's explanation.

I wished I hadn't broken the kaleidoscope X had given me. I wished I could look through it, to see the colours X wanted me to see.

One day, I ripped some of Vincent's postcards. Mama asked me why. I said, "Because he exists."

Either I was a lesbian or the dumbest person on the planet. I couldn't have found a better guy. Why didn't I want him anymore? Why did I want X again? Why did I want to die again?

I started planning another suicide. I thought about going into a forest, taking my clothes off and sleeping under a tree. Freezing to death seemed like an even better idea than drowning. I got immersed in this fantasy and of course in X. The problem was that I remembered so little. I tried so hard to remember her mouth. I strained myself, but I couldn't remember. What kind of love is that?

While I was in the hospital, I read the book Mama bought me, *The Bell Jar*. It's quite depressing. Dr. Hill said maybe it's not a good book to read in my state. I laughed and said the same thing to Dr. Hill that I told Mama. "People don't kill themselves because of books."

In the hospital, I started writing a new book. A book about love, like Mama always wanted. I'm going to write about X and Francis and The Wolf and of course my dear, dear Mama. From then on, I would be preoccupied with writing this book.

I hate Vincent now. I don't know why. I just do. But I want to write about him too, so I stay with him to get more material for my book. This is a fucked up reason to stay with someone, but I thought it was a good reason at the time.

Mama says I began smoking again in the hospital. Poor Mama. Her daughter had a nervous breakdown and went to the hospital to get better. Instead she loses her memory, starts hating the man she loved, and starts smoking again.

I can't remember what Vincent told me about his family. I think his father is dead, but I'm not sure.

These spaces are there because of the ECT, not because the love was so great.

ECT made me forget Vincent's stories about his Mama and Papa, his childhood, his divorce, his dog. They ran through my fingers like water.

Maybe if I didn't have the breakdown, if I wasn't hospitalized and had the ECT, I would've still loved Vincent and we'd be married and living in L.A.

Now, I'm glad I'm with Mama and Papa and our dog. And that I'm a writer.

After the breakdown, being with Vincent was like swallowing my own vomit. I saw Vincent differently. He wasn't a bad man. He didn't scold me or hit me unless I asked him to. He hurt me with his indifference.

Vincent isn't passionate. He doesn't love or hate with fervor. Everything is somewhere along the middle. And I, a manic-depressive, am nowhere near the middle.

I wanted a man with, well, direction. I should have realized this at the very beginning, on Jasper Avenue.

When I was lying next to Vincent, I had terrible thoughts. I wanted to stab him over and over again. I wanted to suffocate him with my pillow. I was too small and too weak.

Before the breakdown, Vincent was perfect, there wasn't a thing wrong with him. Now, so much was wrong. Everything was wrong.

I hated Vincent so much. I fucked him harder and harder. I hoped I would kill him. That he'd have a heart attack.

I'd think, "Vincent you fucking asshole, I fucking hate you, you mother fucker, fucking die, you fucking pig, you dirty old man, you fucking senior citizen, you and your old fucking dick and your gray pubic hair!" It's like I'm fucking my grandfather.

Vincent smelled like old cheese. I wanted him to die. But he was already dead.

He filled me with nothingness. The spaces in him fit into the spaces in me. Together we were like an empty swimming pool.

After the breakdown, all that was left for me was my sexual attraction for Vincent. We were no longer making love, or even having sex. We were "fucking".

My passion didn't come from love. It came from anger and disgust. I wanted to hurt him. Punish him with my fucking.

The more sick and fucked up it was with Vincent, the better. I thought it was okay to do these things with Vincent because he was my boyfriend. This was my excuse.

Once I actually made his penis bleed. Vincent said maybe I should be gentler. I said, "If you don't like it leave." After that he never complained.

What made me really sick was that I still had orgasms. This was awful. These orgasms felt so empty. I hated myself because of these orgasms. The way a victim hates herself if she has an orgasm while she's being raped.

Even though I hated Vincent, a part of me must've still respected him. Because I would never let a person who I didn't respect do these things to me, hurt me like this.

One day, I told Mama I would kill myself if Vincent left me. Mama thought it was because I loved him. She didn't know it was because I needed Vincent to fuck me.

I asked Vincent to spank me. I couldn't tolerate being physically intimate with him otherwise.

I wonder what Mama and Papa would think of me if they knew Vincent spanked me. Each time I asked him to hit harder.

I told Vincent to call me a "whore" and to use the word "cunt". I asked him to rape me.

I didn't want to be raped by a sicko, a criminal, an actual rapist. Vincent was my boyfriend. It was all right when he raped me because I asked him to. This was my logic.

When Vincent was raping me, I begged him to dig his nails into my back. I had scratches on me that looked like I had been attacked by a cougar.

I told Vincent I had hundreds of lovers. They weren't my stories; they were Buddy's. I stole them and passed them off as my own.

Most of the time, I wanted Vincent to fuck me from behind. No, not up the ass. I liked not having to look at him. If you love someone, you probably want to look at them.

I was losing my lost mind. I had crossed so many lines and had gone so far, there was only degeneracy left.

When being spanked wasn't enough, I asked Vincent to slap me across the face. Slaps left red marks, sometimes bruises. Once he accidentally hit my nose and it bled. I looked like a battered wife. Vincent wanted to stop but I insisted we continue. Otherwise, I wouldn't be able to come.

After a while, being loved, being taken care of, didn't matter; only my ability to come. That was my only goal every day, my reason for living.

I became more and more dependent on Vincent, and I hated him because of this. What would I do if Vincent wasn't there to carry out my whims, to spank me or slap me or tie me up or whatever? He was the only man I could do this with, could be myself with.

Once, I thought about urinating on Vincent, but I didn't think he'd go for that. He had limits.

Vincent is well endowed and gets very hard. I wanted to leave him but I stayed because of his penis.

When I asked Vincent why he "cared" for me, he said it was because I was a good person. What the fuck? Here we were having deviant sex, being rough, and talking dirty all the time. Where does me being a good person fit into all this? This had to be bullshit.

Dr. Hill and Mama also said I was good. What's wrong with everyone? Can't they see how bad I am? I'm bad bad bad.

One day, when Vincent was fucking me, I asked him to choke me. He probably thought I wanted to black out, but I actually wanted him to kill me, put me out of my misery.

It wasn't masochism. It was suicide.

I didn't love Vincent. In fact, I hated him. I wanted someone good looking who I hated to fuck me. This is where misery led me.

Dear reader, don't get the wrong idea, that I'd want you to hurt me, rape me. I wouldn't. Those violent fantasies about men in ski masks are just fantasies. I wouldn't want you to put on a ski mask and rape me. This would be awful. I wouldn't enjoy this. Please understand that Vincent was the only man I asked to hurt me like this. He was my boyfriend. I really loved him at first. And he never forced himself on me. I asked him to do these things to me.

When I'm with Vincent, I feel more homosexual than ever. I can't stop thinking about having sex with women.

When Vincent is going down on me, I pretend he's Willow from *Buffy The Vampire Slayer*.

Vincent is masculine. We have intercourse. It's rough, animalistic. Nothing about it reminds me of a woman. But I like it. I want this violence. I can't come without it.

The cunnilingus is wonderful. I need this too.

I need both desperately.

I call a gay help hotline and ask if you can be a lesbian even though you like fucking men. The counselor gave me a complex answer. I hung up.

Since Vincent started to see my deviant side, I decided to tell him I had been with a woman. That I might be bisexual. He was indifferent. I wanted to shock him, but he was like, "That's okay." He wasn't turned on like most men would be.

When I asked him if he would have a ménage à trois with me and another woman, he said, "Only if you do."

Maybe Vincent was the perfect man for me. Maybe I could marry Vincent and still have affairs with women on the side. Maybe Vincent would let me be as fucked up as I wanted to be. Maybe marriage wouldn't be this big normal thing for me. Maybe it would be a life of perversion and deviance.

Vincent said he preferred brunettes. He was amused when I told him I wasn't attracted to women who resembled me, that I couldn't even masturbate in front of the mirror.

He would ask me, "What do you think of her? What about her? And her?" Maybe Vincent thought I fantasized about pussy 24/7.

Who knows what men think? Men are preoccupied with sex and their penises.

Men can't imagine a world without penises. What woman would not want a penis? A penis is what makes sex sex. Bill Clinton thinks the definition of sex is intercourse. For intercourse, you need a penis.

Men think lesbians use dildos or strap-ons. That one of them pretends to be the man.

I never pretended to be "the man". I never wanted a girl to pretend she was "the man".

After I let Vincent read my manuscript, he didn't say much. He said it was "interesting". What people usually say when something is bad or they don't like it.

This hurt. I lost my confidence. I felt talentless. Vincent made me feel like a fucking loser.

I finally understood how Francis had felt when I criticized his poetry. You love someone and you want them to think you're talented and brilliant. You don't want them to say "It's interesting." Or in Francis's case, "It's shit." Yah, maybe I was mean to Francis. But fuck him!

When Vincent told me my writing was interesting, I scratched my nose with my middle finger. Vincent is so clever, he picked up on it right away.

"Amelia, are you giving me the finger?"

"No, I'm scratching my nose," I said. But I was definitely giving him the bird.

I wanted to ask Vincent why he didn't like my writing, but I was afraid his answer would kill me.

Later, when I told him my good news, that I was going to get published, he couldn't believe it. He said I had lucked out.

I can put up with a lot of shit, but I don't need some fucking asshole telling me I am getting published out of luck. It was obvious at that point that Vincent might've thought I was many things, but "brilliant" wasn't one of them.

Good came out of this, dear reader. He motivated me to write, to become a better writer, an artist. I wrote and wrote. More than I had ever written. Out of revenge. Someday Vincent was going to walk into a bookstore and see a book with my name on it, staring at him. He would pick this book up, see my picture on the sleeve, browse through, maybe even read a little. He would know he was defeated, that I had won. I don't need to quote Shakespeare. I have my own words.

Thank you, Vincent, you motherfucking prick.

When we were in Vancouver, Vincent wore the same pair of shorts every day. I remember when we went shopping for jeans, I kept urging him to try a bigger size because you could see his big fat penis and I didn't want him to embarrass Mama when he met her.

He carried six Shakespearian plays with him everywhere he went. When I asked him why he didn't bring more clothes, he said he didn't have any more room in his traveling bag. When I told him he should've brought fewer books with him, he looked at me like I was an idiot.

I wasn't happy in Vancouver with Vincent. I wanted to be home with Mama and Papa and our dog and Dr. Hill. This was my life because of my illness. But I had grown accustomed to this life. I even liked it. Maybe growing up, getting married, and moving out wasn't for me.

Deep down, I didn't want to be someone's wife. I wanted to be Mama's child. Even when I was eighty.

Maybe one day I could live without sex.

Vincent and I walked along the pretty Vancouver shore. I found a piece of driftwood in the shape of a heart, which I later gave to Mama. I held his hand even though I hated him.

Even though I hated him, I wanted to live out a romantic Hallmark card of two lovers holding hands, walking on the beach by the ocean.

When I was writing a postcard to my parents, I asked Vincent to write something too. He wrote, "Thank you." Did he mean "Thank you for giving birth to Amelia" or "Thank you for letting me fuck her"?

One night Vincent started crying. When I asked him why, he said it was because his wife got custody of their dog.

I remembered a line that had worked so well for me before so I used it again. "You disgust me," I said to Vincent. And went to sleep.

All right, divorce was rough, but I seriously doubt that Vincent's life was as tragic as mine. Why should I feel sympathy for him after my horrible life?

For his complaining he deserved to be sodomized. So, I sodomized him with my fingers.

I think he liked it. He didn't complain.

Maybe he was gay.

After Vancouver, Vincent was going to fly back home with me to meet my parents and sisters. He was going to stay with us for a week. Mama went to so much trouble, buying a new bedspread and sheets and setting up a guest room for Vincent.

My sisters couldn't wait to meet Vincent. "Does he really look like Kenneth Branagh?" they asked.

The dirty talking, the spanking, the fucking from behind, the tying up, the raping, wasn't enough. I wanted more. I wanted to share a woman with Vincent. We agreed to proposition a hooker.

We went to the dirty part of town where the street kids hang out. We saw a pretty redhead. Tall, thin, big boobs, about my age. I prefer small boobs but that's okay.

We asked her to come back to our hotel. She said she didn't usually accompany more than one person, that it was dangerous, but we had kind faces and she really needed the money.

We settled on three hundred. The girl came back to our hotel. I fed her, undressed her, bathed her like she was my child. Vincent watched.

She told me about her family and her drug addiction. She ran away from home because her step-father wouldn't keep his hands off her. She shared a small apartment with another prostitute. She was saving up to go to school, maybe to be a dental assistant.

She said she didn't have a pimp, but I didn't believe her. She had bruises all over her, like Francis. When I asked her if she was a hemophiliac, she laughed.

Would you believe, dear reader, that this entire time not once had I asked her what her name was?

I wanted to save her, take her off the streets, and heal her bruises with my love. I wanted to ask her to come live with Vincent and me in L.A. Vincent could be my husband and she could be my wife. She could bear me the children I always wanted.

I sucked on her bumblebee lips and stuck my fingers inside her to feel her temperature. She was hot, burning up. I wanted to taste her.

I fondled her breasts, her ass, her secret garden. I bit her nipples, suckled them eagerly like a hungry new born child.

I let Vincent enter me, fuck me from behind while I masturbated the soft mound of flesh between her legs.

I let her go down on me, explore me with her tongue. Vincent could've been invisible. I felt like I would've done anything for her. I felt she would do anything for me too.

Her skin tasted salty, like seawater. But she was so sweet, like a girl, a young girl. She could have been a virgin, but she'd had hundreds, maybe thousands, of lovers.

God knows I wanted to take her home with me, help her start a new life, but I was ashamed. Not because she was a prostitute; because I couldn't be a lesbian. As much as my mind and body wanted her, as much as I wanted to be a fisherman again, I couldn't.

What if, one day, she didn't want me? What if she left me like X did? I couldn't handle that. It would kill me. What would Mama and Papa say, my sisters? That I died out of love for a woman?

This was the plan: Vincent and I would take this girl back where we found her. Vincent would go home with me to meet my family. Vincent would propose to me. We would get married. And move to L.A. Fuck Chicago!

I had tears in my eyes when we drove her back to the dirty street. She kissed me, a long loving kiss and whispered in my ear, "This doesn't have to be goodbye."

I had the opportunity to save her and, along with saving her, save myself. The voice in my head, be it Mama, God, or my conscience, would not let me be with her.

X was my one woman. I could live with that. Two women would be more than coincidence. Two women would mean bisexuality and border on homosexuality. The idea that I could be attracted to more than one woman, love more than one woman, disturbed me terribly. I didn't have the courage, was not brave enough to openly love women. I couldn't allow myself to be happy with a woman.

I had fallen in love, crazy in love, with this prostitute. If Vincent didn't know this, feel this, see this, hear it in my voice, then he was blind, deaf, and retarded. He was the coldest, most unfeeling, indifferent person on the face of this earth.

I cried all day. I didn't think I could live, go on, without this prostitute. I didn't even know her name. All I knew is that I loved her madly. Her red hair, her swollen lips, even her big boobs.

The next evening I made Vincent drive me to the spot we left her. She wasn't there. We asked around, but no one knew her, knew where she could be. I was so pissed off at myself for not knowing her name, for not taking a picture of her. I prayed she wasn't hurt or dead.

We returned night after night, but there was no sign of her. Nothing. I had lost her.

I wanted her to have a name. So I picked Zowie. I always liked that name. David Bowie named his son Zowie. Zowie Bowie, funny huh?

You never know where you'll find love. I found it in the gutter.

Once you have found it, once it's staring you right in the face, you should be bold, embrace it, not walk away like a coward. Like me.

Maybe it is easier this way. Zowie will always be perfect to me. She will never hurt me like X or my other lovers. I have a perfect mermaid fantasy in my head no one can spoil. No real girl can compete with her. Not even X.

When I got home without Vincent, everyone expected an explanation. I simply said, "Vincent is not for me." Surprisingly, this was enough.

I spent the next month thinking about Zowie, wondering what happened to her, and what could've happened if I had reached out.

What could I have done? Brought her home to live with Mama and Papa? What would I say, "I love this woman who is a prostitute and a drug addict and I want you to provide for her like you've provided for me"?

Could she stop the drugs, the prostitution, the way of life she was accustomed to? What if she was HIV positive? What could I have done and for how long? Maybe

I could've saved her for a minute, but then what? Zowie had one foot in the grave. It was already too late for her. This is what I told myself.

It breaks my heart to think she is selling her beautiful body, having sex with disgusting fat dirty old men. Or that she might be dead in an alley or a dumpster or a pig farm. Maybe I could've been her friend.

I'm glad X changed my mind about prostitutes. She was right.

I stayed in bed in my pajamas, didn't shower and became Smelly Melly. Everyone thought it was because of Vincent, because I missed him. They had no idea I was crying over someone else, a woman.

I felt like a traitor. I wanted to be a normal daughter and a normal sister. I was going to force myself to love a man, to love Vincent. I called Vincent, apologized, said I wanted to try again. He said "Okay." I didn't say I loved him, and he didn't say he loved me.

Everyone was relieved to find out I had made up with Vincent. I got out of my pajamas, took a shower and joined the living.

I had Vincent's phone calls to look forward to again. I convinced myself that this is what I wanted, that I was happy.

It was too much for me to be bisexual. It was easier to be with a man, one man, to get married. I believed if I married Vincent, all my problems would go away. I would never have to worry about sex or love ever again.

I had friends in L.A. and Vincent was going to be in L.A. for business. It was perfect. I could visit my friends, have a rendezvous with Vincent, and put my hands in Natalie Wood's handprints at that famous Chinese Theatre.

In L.A., I asked Vincent to tie me up with a rope. The next day when my friends noticed the rope burn around my wrists, I didn't deny anything. I wanted the world to know I was engaging in heterosexual sex, no matter how kinky or strange. This was my goal: to lead the life of a heterosexual, to be as heterosexual as possible, and to appear heterosexual at all times.

I was going to stick it out with Vincent no matter what. I would endure any annoying habit of his, any thing he said or did that I didn't like.

When I confessed to Vincent I secretly dream of being rich and famous someday, he said all young people dream of that. Vincent always had the ability to make me feel generic.

I told everyone in L.A. I was a writer. Vincent didn't like this. He was like Mama. He thought you weren't a real writer until you were published.

We stood in a lineup to get into the Tonight Show. I asked him to get me a low fat muffin while I waited in line. He came back half an hour later with a fucking bagel. "He can't get anything right," I said to some stranger in the lineup.

I wanted to tell Vincent right there and then to fuck off, to take that bagel and shove it up his ass. I said a low fat muffin! I didn't specify bran, or blueberry, or banana. He had a whole ballpark of flavors to choose from. A bagel is totally different, out of the ballpark, not in the same family. Was I asking for too much? Was I unreasonable to ask for a low fat muffin? If love means having to be content with a bagel when what you asked for is a low fat muffin, love is not for me. Fuck it!

The nice waiter advised us not to order the pork. But fucking Vincent went and ordered it anyway. It was awful whatever it was. It stunk. Maybe it was dog.

Vincent ate every bite on his plate. It was disgusting watching him eat.

My friends were disgusted too. They were all wondering what a girl like me was doing with a shmuck like Vincent. But they didn't know I was crazy. Had they known maybe they would've thought I was lucky.

After this grotesque display, I could never sleep with him again. No matter how big and hard his penis was. It was over.

Later my sisters said there must've been more to it than Chinese food. You don't break up with someone over Chinese food. Especially if you're part Chinese.

Again my parents and sisters asked what happened. Again I said, "Vincent is not for me."

"That's what you said last time," they said.

"Well, this time I'm sure," I said.

I wanted to send Vincent a copy of my book when it was published. But I had liquid papered his phone number.

I missed Vincent. I wished I could bump into him on Jasper Ave again and he'd ask me for directions.

I wanted to try again. This time, no Chinese food.

I can't sleep. I find my phone book. I rub and rub the liquid paper that's on Vincent's number with my nail. It occurs to me to look at the back of the page. I don't know why I didn't think of that earlier. Any way, I can make out the digits. Thank God!

I call Vincent. It's three o'clock in the morning.

"What are you doing?" I ask.

"Sleeping," he says.

In my sexy voice I say, "Vincent, I'm masturbating."

I wait for him to answer. I can hear a woman's voice in the background.

"Can we talk tomorrow?" he says.

"No. Who's that?" I ask.

"My wife. Don't call anymore or I'll call the police."

I hang up. I look in Mama's new secret hiding place. I swallow as many pills as I can. I don't even read the bottles. Some are pink. Some are white. Whatever. I don't care.

I pass out on my bed. Mama finds me unconscious. She and Papa carry me into the car and drive me to the hospital.

I wake up to find a nurse forcing a hose down my esophagus. As they pump my stomach, I gag and cough and struggle for breath. It's so awful.

I will never try to kill myself this way ever again. I've learned my lesson. Next time, I will jump off a building.

When I get home from the hospital, I find Papa's electric shaver. I cut off my long black Chinese hair and shave my head. Then, I step into the shower.

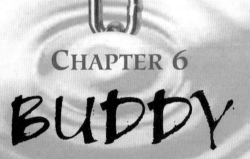

CHAPTER 6
BUDDY

I always wanted what I couldn't have. From the very beginning.

I was always attracted to gay men. There was a space in me for gay men, effeminate men.

When I was twelve, I had posters of George Michael in my room.

He's sweet.
Like licorice.
And chewy.
Black licorice, because he's all black.
Even his eyes.
I can't peer into them.
I don't know what's inside,
And I can't read his mind.
He's so mysterious.
I cut a lock of his black hair as he sleeps.
I use it for a love spell.
His closet is twice the size of mine,
There are only black clothes inside.
He's funny.
So funny sometimes I choke laughing.
Like I'm choking on licorice.
But I want more.
As much as he'll give, and maybe a little more.
I am a criminal.
I steal from him. I steal and steal.
Like the lock of hair while he's asleep.
While we're listening to Gregorian chant music,
While he's dreaming about radiation turning his skin red and making it peel.

I'd like to tell you that I've known Buddy all my life. That we have baby pictures of us naked together. But I've only known him since I was nineteen.

I met Buddy at a straight bar. I was on LSD at the time.

Buddy had long hair. I was confused. Partly because of the LSD and partly because I didn't know if Buddy was a boy or a girl.

I was bold on LSD. So, I kissed Buddy.

He kissed me back. It was an awkward kiss, to say the least. I almost lost a tooth.

We didn't exchange phone numbers because neither of us had a pen. We agreed to meet at the café at 4 o'clock the next day.

This particular café was split into two separate rooms: one smoking and one non. I waited in the smoking section. I was sure he had said smoking. And I think I remember him smoking.

I waited two hours but Buddy didn't show up.

Two months later, I bumped into him at a gay bar. I told him I had waited in the smoking section. He said there had been a mix up, that he had waited in the non-smoking section for forty-five minutes.

Years later, he confessed he never went to the café.

Buddy was weak, and always cold, like there was no life in him.

Loving Buddy was like loving a ghost. I was grasping for what couldn't be grasped. There was no shape, no substance.

Maybe Buddy was caught between worlds: the living and the non-living.

Maybe Buddy wasn't human. Maybe he had no soul. Maybe he was nothing. Maybe I loved nothing.

Sometimes, I wondered if Buddy was a figment of my imagination, my invisible friend, if I had created him out of my loneliness.

Buddy was thin. Mama thought he looked sick. I envied him.

He was the closest thing to a real vampire. I think he read too many Anne Rice books. Buddy was the kind of person you could see working with the dead.

Like reading *The Bell Jar*, Mama thought hanging around Buddy would make me more depressed, push me over the edge.

Mama liked Buddy. But she didn't think that her daughter, her sick daughter, should be around such a depressed, suicidal individual.

And what if this boy who practiced sodomy had Bluekemia or something? What if her daughter drank from the same glass? What if she kissed him on the mouth? What if she got drunk and had sex with this boy?

Poor Mama didn't know her daughter didn't need to get drunk to sleep with that boy. And Mama didn't know that that boy also drank people's blood.

To say that Buddy wasn't normal is an understatement. We weren't sure he was human.

Buddy was an ugly baby. So ugly, his mother said that when he came out of her, she was scared. She wouldn't breastfeed him.

Buddy's mother kept Buddy in the house, hidden away. He never had a tan in his entire life.

He wouldn't go fishing with me. He didn't even go outside to walk his dog.

Buddy never went swimming. He hated his body. He was hunched over and not very tall, but he was the most beautiful boy I'd ever known. Except for Manuel. Like there was only one Jesus, there was only one Manuel.

Buddy was an inch away from being a cripple. He walked with a limp, one of his legs was shorter than the other, and he had scoliosis. He wouldn't wear a back brace, and his parents didn't love him enough to force him to wear one. Mama would have made me wear one.

Along with his other numerous flaws, Buddy alsohad crooked teeth. Not only did he refuse to wear a back brace, but he refused to wear braces on his teeth. His parents said nothing.

On top of everything, Buddy had a lazy eye. I know, I know: how can a person have so many flaws and yets be so attractive? Well, Lord Byron had a club foot, but that didn't stop him from being a Casanova.

Buddy was so many wrongs that somehow made a right.

He was a disaster area. Someone should put some orange pylons around him and tape that says "Hazard".

Maybe it's this culture. We accept freaks like Buddy with his cape and his limp. If he were in Blueland, people would throw money at him.

Poor Buddy. What kind of parents were they? To not make him wear a back brace, braces, or glasses. Didn't they care at all? These are horrible, horrible people!!!

Buddy hated birthdays. You weren't even allowed to mention his.

Our birthdays are three days apart. For our twenty-fifth birthday, we almost drove off a cliff like Thelma and Louise. In the end, we decided just to rent the movie.

Buddy said he had a big knife under his bed. He phoned me at 3 o'clock in the morning to tell me he was going to use it. I begged him not to. I told him he was going to meet Madonna one day. He went to sleep. But he phoned again the next week or the next month or on his birthday.

Buddy and I loved to talk about death. I want to drown like Natalie Wood. He wanted to die in a car crash like James Dean. I wondered which one of us would die first.

Buddy thought there was something sexual about a car crash. That the speed and intensity would induce an orgasm. A man would get an erection, ejaculate in his pants.

I hope poor Manuel had an orgasm.

Buddy thought that surviving a car crash would be thrilling too. To experience such an impact and not cross over.

One Hallowe'en, Buddy wore an eye patch and a leg brace, and walked with a cane. He went as a car accident victim.

He had sex with three people that night. He said it was the most erotic thing he'd ever done.

The funny part is, Buddy didn't drive.

After Buddy tried to kill himself by overdosing on sleeping pills (he was stupid like me), Mama and Papa forbade me to see him.

I didn't listen. I had my way. I always had my way. That is the good thing about being depressed. People feel sorry for you and let you have your way.

When I think of Buddy, I don't just think of one solitary person. Buddy was a door to another world for me.

The gays, bisexuals, transvestites, transsexuals, the rebels, and the freaks. I've labelled this period of my life "The Buddy Years".

I was a dancing queen during The Buddy Years. I preferred gay bars. They played the best music and gay men were the best dancers. They were gorgeous. Some danced without their shirts on.

I made out with more gay men at gay bars than straight men at straight bars. The lesbians stared at me like I was the enemy.

I was strictly a fag hag. I went for the men, not the women. Gay men are wonderful. They want to dance with me, kiss me, shop with me. Some asked me to have their children. Those gay men made me feel more attractive than any straight man did.

I never went further than oral sex, though. I was afraid of disease. Mama had put the fear in me. And it wasn't just gay men; it was all men.

Also, because I didn't have intercourse, I didn't feel like a slut. I felt innocent. Like Bill Clinton.

When my sisters found out I was going to gay bars, they thought I was going to end up gay. But like a book doesn't drive you to kill yourself, a gay bar doesn't make someone gay. Lots of straight people go and stay straight.

When I look at a woman, I don't think "Gee, I'd like to fuck her." However, I can become emotionally attracted to a woman and a sexual attraction can develop from that.

I do have sexual thoughts about men when I first see them, but the longer I know them the less attractive they are to me.

Maybe I'm sexually heterosexual and emotionally homosexual.

Gay men are sensitive like women. My attraction to them makes sense. I'm sexually and emotionally attracted to them.

Buddy says I should be with a hermaphrodite, but I'd sooner fuck a man with no legs.

I felt my self splitting. One Amelia existed in Mama's world and one in Buddy's.

I liked the idea of having a double identity. I told everyone at the gay bar to call me "Mel". This was before Mel B. and Mel C. of The Spice Girls became famous.

Buddy thought "Mel" was butchy. He called me "Melly" and later on "Smelly Melly". I hated being called that, but now I miss it. It's strange what we will miss.

Buddy's real name was Frederick. Only his mother called him that. I wanted to call him "Bud", but he wouldn't let me.

I called all my friends "Buddy". It was funny to me that it was somebody's name, but it fit. Buddy became my best buddy.

I remember the first time I introduced X to Buddy. We had some beer. We went outside and made snow angels. I couldn't believe Buddy went outside.

When Buddy asked X how old she was, she said "27 or 28." Later, Buddy said to me in private, "What does she mean, 'or'?"

X was jealous of Buddy. She suspected we were having an affair. X was pretty jealous for someone who claimed not to be a jealous person.

Buddy was obsessed with Charles almost as much as I was with X. Charles had big bulging eyes like a goblin, but he was attractive to Buddy because he made Buddy suffer. He would not tell Buddy he loved him, and I think Buddy enjoyed this pain.

Buddy hated Christmas. Christmas music made him depressed, suicidal.

One Christmas, Buddy bought Charles a three hundred dollar black sweater. Charles bought him a Christmas songs CD. Buddy listened to it to torture himself.

I kept telling Buddy to end it. We'd have two-hour phone conversations in which I would convince him that Charles was all wrong for him, that Buddy should dump Charles before Charles dumped him. Buddy would thank me and tell me I was his best friend.

The next day, Buddy would always change his mind. Buddy accused me of trying to break them up. He said Charles was the only source of happiness in his life, and that I wanted to take that away from him.

Buddy was studying to be a librarian. His dream was for him and Charles to move to a small town no-one ever heard of, and for Buddy to work in an old haunted library.

Buddy called Charles "Bastard". I had an "X" and Buddy had a "Bastard".

Charles was a virgin when he met Buddy. They say there's nothing sweeter than a virgin. How could I compete?

Also, Charles was a professional pianist.

There wasn't a piano in their apartment. Charles went to his parents' house to practice. Poor Buddy never got to hear Charles play.

Buddy's twin died at birth.

Buddy believed everyone had a double. That somewhere out there there was someone who looked just like you.

When I asked Buddy what he would do if he met his double, he said he would fuck him.

If there were two Buddys, I'd want to fuck both of them at the same time. It would be the best ménage-à-trois ever.

Someone once said that if you love someone so intensely, they probably love you too. I disagree. There are a lot of psychos out there who are in love with, say, Winona Ryder. And Winona doesn't love them back, doesn't even know they exist.

Buddy had a tattoo of an eye on his back, yet for years he couldn't see that I was enamoured with him.

I offered to let Buddy sodomize me. I even offered to let him drink my blood, but he turned me down.

When we went to the gay bar I was not allowed to kiss him or hug him. Not to scare off any of his potential suitors.

When we were alone, I touched him all the time. His skin was smooth, like a girl's. He'd never done any labour in his life.

Once, he took guitar lessons. He quit when he got calluses.

Buddy never used public washrooms. He was afraid of getting Bluekemia. He was like Mama: Mama is always telling me not to use public washrooms, to hold it.

Buddy was convinced people got Bluekemia from drinking tap water. He only drank bottled water or mineral water. I thought Buddy was paranoid.

Buddy's most painful secret was that he was a bedwetter. He peed in his sleep until he was well into his teens. His mother told me when she was drunk.

His parents didn't take him to see a psychologist.

Apart from Buddy's flaws and my fat, we looked like brother and sister. Maybe this was the problem. Incest.

I think Buddy saved me after I learned the truth about Vincent. Mama was my breath, but Buddy kept me afloat.

Buddy was also depressed. But I was more depressed. Buddy let me be more depressed. He let me be the most depressed person on the planet. I loved him for that.

Buddy and I are big ABBA fans. We were going to form a band with just the two of us. Buddy would play keyboard and I would sing and play guitar. Amelia and Buddy. We'd be like ABBA, except without the BA.

Buddy probably had a hundred lovers. Half of them were girls. Who knows how many children he has fathered?

There was a period when I wanted to have Buddy's child. When I was willing to risk having a sick baby.

I thought if I was going to have a child with anyone, it would be Buddy. But if Buddy's and my genes were combined, we'd have a very depressed individual on our hands. I could just see this child saying, "Mama, how could you?"

Buddy used to say "Streets are straight. Not people." He said everyone is innately bisexual, that we are attracted to the person not the gender.

I preferred it when Buddy was strictly homosexual. I knew I couldn't compete with someone who had different plumbing. It was harder for me when he had female lovers. I wanted to tear my hair out. But, after Vincent, there was nothing to tear out.

After Buddy's sister got raped, he turned completely gay. Or so he said.

Buddy liked violent sex. But being violent towards women made him feel like a rapist. So, he turned his aggression towards men. Now, Buddy's father hates him.

Buddy's father is a total loser. He was caught shoplifting cough medicine. He paid Buddy to stay out of his life. Buddy told people his father was dead.

Buddy spent a lot of time in bed wearing only pantyhose, watching porn, and masturbating.

With all the masturbating Buddy did, you'd think the energy would keep flowing, that he'd never get a disease.

Buddy said he didn't like fucking all that much. He liked foreplay, but actual fucking was a disappointment.

Buddy said sex being so good is all hype. Buddy thought people are being brainwashed, that the condom companies are behind it.

Buddy said sex exists mainly for procreation. Sometimes I thought Buddy sounded like an old-fashioned 1950's housewife.

When I asked him what the point of homosexuality is, he said "It's a political statement."

Buddy's favourite singer was Madonna. When he turned completely gay, he said she was the only woman he would have sex with.

Buddy was going to send Madonna's fan club a letter saying he had cancer and his dying wish was to meet Madonna. But Buddy didn't want to stoop to Francis' level.

Buddy disliked all my lovers, but he disliked Francis the most.

I flirted with Charles a little.

Buddy warned me not to play games. It was the first time Buddy scared me. You wouldn't want to get on Buddy's bad side. In high school, he got revenge on his girlfriend by putting a dead rat in her locker. And a death threat written in blood.

Charles had driven Buddy mad.

Buddy spent several months in the psych ward. Buddy was the only friend I had who had been there. Maybe that's why I felt so close to him.

I was jealous that Charles had this effect on Buddy. I wished Buddy loved me enough to go crazy for me.

I was a silly girl. Chasing a gay man, trying to make him jealous with other gay men.

Mama says a woman can't change a man. She tried to change Papa.

At one point, Buddy and I almost moved in together. We talked about it a lot. But Buddy changed his mind at the last minute.

Now, when I look back, I think he never wanted to live with me.

I think he feared me, suspected I wanted more than friendship.

Perhaps it was I who was the rapist.

Buddy said there are two kinds of people: those who like showers and those who like baths. Shower people should be with shower people and bath people should be with bath people. By no means should the two mix.

Maybe the problem wasn't that Buddy was gay. Maybe the problem was that I liked showers and Buddy liked baths.

Buddy sponsored a child in Africa. Buddy wrote him letters. I don't know what he wrote, only that he told him he was gay. Buddy was out to everyone, even this child in Africa.

Buddy was obsessive compulsive. He was particularly anal about his socks and underwear. They were all black. If there was any discolouration after washing, out they went. I swear he bought new socks and underwear every week. He must have spent half his paycheque on socks and underwear.

Buddy liked to cook and clean. When he was depressed, he cleaned his entire house.

Buddy said one's house was a reflection of one's self. Buddy and Mama had this much in common.

Buddy was such a clean freak, I thought for sure he'd end up dating someone in the medical field.

When he went to the doctor, he pretended to have pain in his penis and anus so he would get examined. He hoped the doctor would take advantage of him.

He'd come back from his check-up and proudly declare that the doctor told him to cut down on anal sex.

Buddy couldn't eat beef. He said it was because cows had sad eyes.

I guess he's right. They do have rather sad eyes. Maybe they're depressed. Maybe they should be on antidepressants.

Maybe when I'm eating beef, I'm eating depression. And thus becoming more depressed. Maybe depressed people shouldn't eat beef. Maybe depressed people shouldn't live in Alberta.

Maybe people are doing cows a favour by killing them. Maybe we're putting them out of their misery.

Buddy was one of those people who constantly thought about nuclear war. He was convinced Canada was going to bomb Blueland and the planet was going to be contaminated with radiation.

If Buddy had cancer, he would refuse to go for radiation treatment. Like he refused the back brace, the braces, and the glasses.

I'm superstitious. It's the Blue in me. The Blue are very superstitious people.

Buddy made fun of me for being superstitious.

Buddy and Charles exchanged toe rings.

When Buddy lost his, Charles broke up with him.

Later, Buddy moved to Calgary, went to school, got his license and bought a car.

I confessed to Buddy that I always hated Charles, that I wished I could pluck out his big bulging eyes and preserve them in a jar of water. Buddy said nothing.

Buddy was addicted to the news. He loved hearing about all the bad stuff happening in the world. It made his life bearable.

I was the first person he told what plane crashed, where there was an earthquake or a hurricane, and of course what murders were committed. This made me feel special. Like when The Wolf talked to me about politics.

When Buddy was four, he got lost in a mall. He thought his mother left him on purpose. She probably did, but changed her mind. Out of fear of going to hell.

She waited two days to claim her son. It was all over the newspapers. Buddy had his fifteen minutes of fame.

Buddy said being deserted by his mother was worse than being fondled by his uncle.

Buddy didn't think his molestation fucked him up. Often, damaged people don't know they're damaged.

I wonder if Buddy got an erection when his uncle fondled him. I know this is a sick thought, but it's a thought. Maybe that's why Buddy was gay.

Buddy once said that everyone secretly wants to relive their abuse. Except this time to be in control, to have the power. So if a man did it to you, you want a man. If a fat man did it to you, then you want a fat man.

But I didn't want a fat man. Maybe I was a backward girl.

When I stayed over at Buddy's, we shared the same bed. He slept in the nude. This was the closest I got to having sex with him.

Nothing happened. No accidental brush against my nipple. Nothing.

I doubt he ever got an erection around me. I was Smelly Melly. Not Sexy Melly or Irresistible Melly. I think Buddy would've sooner fucked one of his cousins.

There was no danger of being raped. Yet I still had hope.

When I watched Buddy sleep, I wanted to kiss his eyelids, lick his eyelashes. Buddy had the longest eyelashes. The drag queens were jealous. There were rumours Buddy's eyelashes were fake, but I didn't believe this.

There were also rumours that Buddy used to draw on fake sideburns with black eyeliner. This I believed.

Buddy has a hundred Charles stories and I have my handful of X stories.

We'd light candles, open a bottle of red wine, and drink and talk all night about how despicable Charles and X were. How they jilted us and left us with no other alternative but to kill ourselves.

One night, Buddy put a curse on Charles. He vowed Charles would wander the earth loveless.

Buddy offered to put a curse on X. It was tempting, but I was too scared of the repercussions, that it would come back tenfold. I told Buddy that sodomizing my Barbie doll was enough for me.

For Hallowe'en, I asked Buddy if he could fuck me if I wore a mask, if I pretended to be a boy. He wouldn't.

Were my buttocks so different from a boy's?

Papa told me about a Blueland myth that if you reached the other side of the rainbow you would change genders.

How I wanted to go over the rainbow and turn into a boy for Buddy.

Buddy once told me he wished he could be a girl. I told Buddy what Papa told me. When he got high, he'd yell "Let's go over the rainbow, Melly. Let's go!"

I rarely did street drugs. I had a phobia. If I didn't know exactly what was in it, I didn't swallow it. So I abused my meds. They felt safe because Dr. Hill had prescribed them.

I mixed my prescription drugs with alcohol. And of course I shared with Buddy.

I remember sleeping over at Buddy's and not knowing how many pills I had taken, wondering if I would never wake up.

Buddy didn't believe in religion. "Fuck religion," he said.

Buddy thought that when you die, the worms eat your eyes and you decompose. You become fertilizer. That's it.

It's over. You don't feel anything. You don't think anything. You enter a state of nothingness.

Buddy was such a card.

When Mormons knocked on Buddy's door, he told them he was a Satanist.

When people were collecting for charities, he told them he spent all his money on drugs and gambling.

When a vacuum cleaner salesman came, he told him he liked dust. But he took the free knife set.

That was Buddy for you.

Buddy's mother is nice, but flaky. She thinks aliens are trying to contact her. When we had a little party, she got plastered and danced around in her underwear.

I had some good conversations with Buddy's mother. She didn't believe Buddy was completely gay either. She even thought he'd marry a girl someday. I didn't tell her I hoped to be that girl.

Buddy's mother sewed him a cape. He wore it on special occasions or to the gay bar.

Mama thought Buddy was weird. "Why is he wearing a cape?" she would ask.

Afterwards, she referred to him as "Dracula". It was always "Dracula's on the phone" or "Dracula's here."

Like his mother, Buddy believed in aliens. He convinced me I was from another planet. He said all manic-depressives are from another planet. It took me years of Earthling therapy before I started to believe I was an Earthling again.

Buddy burned himself with cigarettes. Sometimes he cut himself too. He made Francis' cuts look like paper cuts.

One time he was making love to Charles and he slashed his arm. He had to get forty-six stitches. He let me touch his stitches. They felt like fish scales.

I wished I could give Buddy the pain he longed for, but I loved Buddy too much. I couldn't even pinch him.

In the winter, I'm so depressed. I daydream about summer in Blueland. When I was eight years old and didn't have to wear a bikini top and the only thing on my mind was getting a tan.

Buddy liked winter. I think it was his excuse to stay inside.

Buddy never let me photograph him. But my mind took plenty of Polaroids. Buddy in his cape, Buddy smoking, Buddy frowning. A lot of Buddy frowning.

I have these pictures to comfort me. Not like the shifting face of X that tortures me. Why did the ECT erase X and not Buddy?

Buddy's favourite game was Monopoly. We played for real money. Buddy owes me $1,237,500,000.00.

There was nothing more in the world that Buddy liked to do than take a shit. And he loved talking about it. He'd always tell me if it was a good one or not, if he had to strain himself.

Buddy was so thoughtful. He'd always ask me how my menstrual flow was. I don't think I'll ever have a more thoughtful friend than Buddy.

I don't smoke, except when I'm with Buddy. I love smoking with Buddy. We smoke Marlboros.

Buddy looks great when he smokes a cigarette. Like a movie star.

I wanted my publishers to put a photo of me smoking on the back of my book, but they said no.

In Blueland, the fucking tombstones have pictures of the people smoking. I remember saying to Mama, "But what if they died of lung cancer?"

One summer day, Buddy and I ate a huge watermelon all by ourselves. We put vodka in it.

When a drunken Buddy asked to see my seed-filled feces, I started to cry.

Buddy was a waiter. When he got fired from a restaurant, I helped him get his revenge. I released forty-two crickets (the pet store didn't have cockroaches) in the bathroom of the restaurant.

This was the only crime I've ever committed.

Buddy spied on his seventy-year-old neighbour. He videotaped him doing yoga in a leotard. Buddy sold copies of the video at the gay bar for $20 a pop.

Buddy said he didn't feel bad because the old man was probably a pervert. All old men are perverts. I didn't argue. Buddy could have gone big time with the video stuff, but he was afraid of going to jail. Not because he'd be everyone's bitch, but because jail would be so dirty. It was the thought of a prison toilet that kept Buddy from breaking the law.

Buddy liked Jeremy Irons first. His favourite Jeremy Irons film was *Dead Ringers*, where Jeremy played twin gynecologists. You know how I said fondling Francis in a movie theatre began out of boredom? Well, actually, I stole it from Buddy. He told me that's what he used to do to Charles.

I also became a vegetarian because of Buddy.

Buddy was a terrible ventriloquist. He made a puppet with black hair and black clothes and called him "Little Buddy". When people came over, he'd bring Little

Buddy out and have conversations with him. I let Little Buddy sodomize my X Barbie doll. Once I accidentally sat on Little Buddy. It almost ended our friendship.

Buddy said Little Buddy was from Dimension 5 and was gay too. One day, Buddy said, Little Buddy was going to kill someone with a little knife. I told Buddy to call Dr. Hill.

I could be as crazy and deviant as I wanted with Buddy. Buddy had tried everything, and we had no secrets. Or so I thought.

Then, one day, I saw a picture of Buddy with blond hair in his photo album. "When did you dye your hair blond?" I asked.

Then Buddy told me the truth, the horrid truth. Buddy was a natural blond. My jaw dropped. Oh, my God!!!

Buddy was actually wearing colour in the picture. He was wearing a green shirt.

Ever since I'd known Buddy, he was dark and dismal. I assumed he was always this way. I never thought he had been blond and worn green.

Maybe I was the only completely dark and dismal person on the planet. Dark and dismal from birth. Maybe even Marilyn Manson had a light period.

Buddy never went out for recess. His mother wrote the teacher a note saying that Buddy was allergic to the sun. Buddy told me how much he wished he could have gone outside and played Double Dutch.

I borrowed a skipping rope from Buddy's neighbours and asked his Mama if she could turn the rope with me.

Buddy skipped for one hour straight, without a mistake.

We even made him a crown out of tinfoil and crowned him the king of Double Dutch.

Buddy played the lottery every week. He'd buy, like, thirty tickets. I'd say, "Buddy, with your teeth, your back, your eye, do you really think you're lucky, that you're going to win?"

I don't think so.

Buddy carried a First Aid kit wherever he went, even to the gay bar. One time, a drunk fell and got hurt. Buddy cleaned the wound and bandaged him.

Buddy had more shoes than anyone I've ever known. They were all black and pretty much looked the same.

When we went to Calgary together, he bought a dozen pairs. We were visiting for only a couple of days. What did he need all those shoes for?

X was performing in Calgary that weekend. The day before, X and I had a huge fight and I was convinced X would sleep with her dancer whore again.

Buddy and a few of his friends were going down to Calgary. When Buddy asked me to come along, I jumped at the opportunity. I thought it was destiny.

When we got there, I phoned X's mother's house. The dancer whore answered the phone and told me to fuck off. I told Buddy's friends I was going to break the dancer whore's leg and asked if anyone wanted to join me. Sabrina volunteered. She brought a camera.

We drove to X's mother's house. I rang the bell. When no-one answered, I banged on the door and yelled "Come out, you carpet licker, you lesbian whore!"

When I didn't get an answer, I dropped my drawers and urinated on X's mother's doorstep. Sabrina took a picture.

Then we went to a bakery, bought a chocolate cake, and had the baker write in pink icing "Congradulations, your daughter is a lezzzbian." I was going to have the cake delivered when X's mother returned home. Now, that is revenge.

Sabrina took a picture of me kissing the cute Italian baker on the cheek. His name was Mario. Boy, was he hot! I considered seducing Mario in the bakery and having Sabrina take pictures of our naked bodies sprawled on the counter.

When the store's piped-in music started playing my song, our song, mine and X's, I sobbed like a baby. I couldn't go through with the plan.

Sabrina thought I was pathetic for wimping out. Everyone did, especially Buddy. I could have had a fucking awesome revenge. Buddy said he expected more from a person who released forty-two crickets in a restaurant.

I shared my cake with everyone, but I ate the "lezzz" piece. Sabrina took a picture of me eating it.

Buddy said that at least I had good writing material.

When X left me, Buddy's wish came true: we had a car accident. It was raining and I pressed down on the brake a half second too late. We slid and hit a car in front of us. Neither one of us was seriously hurt. There were no broken bones or spilled blood. Buddy was disappointed.

I remember calling X and telling her I was nearly killed, and being so close to death, I realized God wanted us to be together. She hung up on me.

When I saw the picture of X in a wedding dress in the newspaper with her head flung back, Buddy said we should go to the performance. To see if she sucks.

"We could jinx her and make her fall," he said.

"I'm exhausted," I said.

"Who are you and what have you done to my Smelly Melly?" Buddy asked.

When I was on lithium, Buddy begged me for a bottle. I didn't have any to spare. I was saving up.

I think he was planning his suicide, but I was too busy planning my own.

I asked Buddy to kill me, so I wouldn't have to go to hell. Buddy was an atheist, so he didn't have to worry about hell.

I said, "If you love me, you'll do it." I remembered hearing those words before.

When I finally told Buddy I loved him, was in love with him, he said I was just lonely, on the rebound from Vincent. Besides, it could never be, could never ever be. I wasn't a man.

I was upset. It's not like he was 100% gay.

Buddy said if I pushed him, I would ruin our friendship. And me being me, I pushed.

One day, we were watching porn together. Hetero porn. Why is Buddy watching this with me if he is so gay? Is he drunk?

Then we dance to Peggy Lee's "Fever". I try to kiss him. He backs away. I put my hand on his crotch. Buddy burns me with his cigarette.

There would be no more Thelma and Louise.

I couldn't believe Buddy would hurt me like that. I called him a faggot. I went into the kitchen and grabbed a knife. I threatened to stab myself. Buddy took the knife away from me and said "Let me do it."

He told me to get undressed and hop into his bed. He handcuffed me to his bedpost and left me alone. I waited and waited. I thought he was going to come back and make passionate love to me.

After an hour, he returned and let me go.

I just wanted him to try. I would've tried for him. It was me, his "Smelly Melly". If I was his best friend, he fucking owed it to me to try.

Buddy just kept saying, "I can't, I can't."

I kept asking, "Why not? Why not?"

Most of Buddy's female lovers looked like me: petite, blue eyes, black hair.

If he could sleep with them, why not me? Dear Lord, why not me? It must be the fat.

His friends said I was one of those women who think they can change a gay man. I didn't see Buddy as a gay man. I thought Buddy was a fish like me.

Before I left, I took my Chris Isaak CD. I noticed that not only did Buddy have Peggy Lee, but there was also Judy Garland, Liza Minnelli, Barbra Streisand, Bette Midler, and Cher. Maybe Buddy was completely gay after all.

Every time I saw someone walking downtown wearing all black, I'd turn around. My neck got pretty sore.

It was hard without Buddy. In the end, it was for the best. I stopped talking about X and Francis and Vincent. I was cured of my obsession.

I was like an addict in rehab, wanting to talk about my old lovers but not being able to. Dr. Hill said abstinence, from Buddy, was the key to recovery.

I avoided places Buddy went to. Gay bars, gay cafes, bath houses, vegetarian restaurants. I started eating meat again. All of a sudden I craved meat. Not bloody meat. Well cooked. Mama said I was coming to my senses.

Buddy has a phobia of styrofoam. If you want to make him cry, squish some styrofoam. The sound will drive Buddy batty.

After he burned me, I sent him a box of styrofoam. To a normal person this would seem innocent. To Buddy this was a declaration of war.

I had diarrhea for three days straight. I knew it was Buddy's doing. Whenever someone pissed Buddy off, he would put a spell on them that they would have diarrhea.

I wondered if Buddy ever asked about me, if he cared whether or not I was dead.

I wanted to call him. I would pick up the phone, dial, and hang up when he answered. I was turning into Francis.

When I could no longer tolerate Buddy's absence, I went to the gay bar. I ran into Sabrina.

"Buddy's dead," she said. "He had Bluekemia...everyone knew."

Maybe it was a joke. Maybe this was Buddy's revenge. I went to the gay bar night after night, but Buddy wasn't on the dance floor.

There are so many "should've" and "could've". There is so much bullshit.

Buddy shouldn't have hurt me the way he did. He could've said he was sorry. Now that he's dead, it all feels like my fault. I am a true Bluelander: I absolve the dead of all blame.

I should've been there for Buddy. He must have thought I'd call. I should've called. His Smelly Melly should've held his cold hand as he was dying in that fucking hospital bed.

I could've made him laugh. I could've told him how lucky he was to die, that he was a bastard for beating me to it. He would have liked to hear that.

Like I said: should've...could've...bullshit.

Maybe Buddy wouldn't make love to me because he wanted to spare me. Maybe if he hadn't had Bluekemia, he would have been my lover, wouldn't have burned me with his cigarette. Maybe Brenda Lee put him in the mood too.

Buddy could've given me the death I so desired.

I wish I could bury Buddy in Blueland, get him a lovely tombstone, give him a big fat Blue funeral. Buddy was the kind of person who fantasized about his funeral all the time. But he would be funeral-less.

I'm glad I'm Blue. The Blue respect the dead. We know how to put on a proper funeral. We settle only for the best, most expensive, tombstone.

When I tell my Mama, Papa, and my sisters that Buddy is dead, they say it's too bad, that he was too young. Even that he was a nice boy. This last part surprises me a bit, but they are Blue, after all. Death changes everything for the Blue. The truth changes. The bad become good and the ugly become beautiful. The dead are transformed into something they could never be in life.

A month later, Buddy's sister called me and said Buddy had left something for me. I thought it was his cape. When I went over, she led me to Buddy's room and opened his closet. Inside were dozens and dozens of plastic containers filled with what looked like old semen.

Why had Buddy left me his semen? Was this semen infected with Bluekemia? Was Buddy's gift to me death?

Buddy's sister also showed me a box with Buddy's writing inside. "Here's some crap," she said.

I didn't know Buddy wrote. It was beautiful. Better than Vincent's love letters, better than Francis' poetry. I thought Francis was the real poet, but it was Buddy all along.

Besides the semen and the box of poetry, the only thing I had left of Buddy was the scar from the cigarette burn. Now this seemed beautiful, too. Buddy had left his mark on me; I didn't want it to ever fade.

I tell Dr. Hill I was a bad friend to Buddy. He was getting paler and paler, thinner and thinner. Mama said he looked sick, but I didn't notice. He looked like the same old Buddy to me.

We ate at Papa's Chinese restaurant every day. The food was a little salty, but it was free. My best friend was deteriorating before my eyes, but I couldn't see. What kind of person doesn't notice their best friend is dying? Especially when I, too, was dying – only for me it was not in body but in spirit.

I saw the Buddy I always saw: the vampire. Vampires are pale and thin. Like Buddy.

I didn't see that Buddy was ill, like no-one saw what The Wolf was doing to me. Finally I understood how Mama and Papa must feel.

Did he know when we were plotting our deaths? Did he want to die because he knew he was sick? Maybe while Buddy was saying he wanted to die, to be in a car crash, he really wanted to live. Maybe Buddy was the opposite of me. Maybe while I desperately wanted to die, he desperately wanted to live.

I'm not sure, but I think Buddy always used condoms. Like Mama, he feared disease. My guess is that he got Bluekemia from drinking his lovers' blood. Buddy loved the taste of blood. He'd been drinking blood since he was a little kid and a girl hurt herself on the monkey bars. Buddy sucked her arm to stop it from bleeding.

Buddy said he was a vampire. I don't know if he truly believed this. I don't know how deluded he was. Real vampires are immortal, and Buddy wasn't.

One day, I bumped into X's friend, Matt. I hadn't seen Matt in five years. I was flabbergasted when he gave me a hug and said he'd bought my book.

I liked Matt, but, as you've probably guessed dear reader, I had an ulterior motive. I wanted to find out about X: who was she sleeping with, where was she living, if she ever talked about me. I never asked. I waited for Matt to mention something first.

If Mama knew I was friends with X's friend, she would say I was looking for trouble. But I couldn't foresee any problems with Matt.

One night, Matt and I went to a bar. We had some nachos and beer. When I went to the washroom, Matt must have slipped something into my drink. I think I see Buddy, but Buddy's dead. Unless it's his twin.

The next thing I know, I am tired and drowsy and it's blurry and I am being raped by Matt in his car.

Thank God Mama made me carry condoms in my purse! Matt was nice enough to put one on when I asked.

He even drove me home like a real gentleman. He said if I ever felt depressed or lonely to give him a call. That he would fuck the depression out of me, that all I needed was a good fuck now and then. He'd be happy to provide this service.

In a way it felt like a regular date. Matt picked me up, we grabbed a bite, had a drink, and Matt drove me home. The only thing out of place was Matt drugging and raping me.

When I got home, I took a shower. A two-hour-long shower to wash off all the slime. Then I slept for twelve hours straight. I wanted to sleep and forget.

The first thing I did when I got up was to take another long shower, just in case some slime was left over.

Then, after Mama made me my espresso, she told me the bad news: our beloved dog was ill and the vet recommended we put him down soon.

Under normal circumstances, I would have been devastated. Since I had just been raped, I was okay with this. It even made sense, that something so bad would happen then.

I didn't cry. I just said, "We can't let him suffer." Mama thought I was numb because I was in shock. She couldn't guess her daughter had just been raped.

I wondered how I would go on without that fur and that fat. I loved that fat. It was the only fat I ever loved.

I showered three times a day. Papa said he wouldn't be able to afford the water bill. I scrubbed and I scrubbed. I had to get rid of any particle of Matt that might be left on me. I wanted to scrub Matt out.

I liked Matt. I really did. Now I hate him, and I hate myself for not knowing any better. For not being able to spot a wolf. You'd think I would be able to sniff one out by now. I feel like I deserved to be raped. Dr. Hill says there is no such thing as deserving to be raped.

After I was raped, I felt calm. The worst had happened to me and I had survived. It didn't kill me as I always thought it would.

I think once you're raped you stay raped. The experience becomes a part of you, for better or worse. It's unshakeable. The therapists will tell you you will recover, you will be able to put it in the past. What they don't tell you is that no matter how deep you bury it, it will haunt you, even in the smallest way. When you're making love, it will be there, somewhere, in the back of your mind.

But maybe we're the lucky ones. We don't have to be afraid every day, everywhere we go, of everyone we meet. Mama was one of those women: always telling me not to talk to strangers, not to be alone with teachers, to stay away from older boys.

It's a big price to pay. But I no longer fear the unknown.

A week later, Matt phoned me like nothing had happened. I thought he wanted to fuck me again. I hung up on him. He called again.

Does he think I am the stupidest girl in the world and I don't know what rape is?

Matt belongs in prison. I should sue him. I should call the police. But the police will probably say that a girl who writes about fucking probably led Matt on. I'm fucked because I write about fucking. I can get raped over and over again and they will say the same thing: "This girl writes about fucking."

I feel like the word rape should have a "z" sound in it, like crazzzy and lezzzbian.

Matt isn't handsome, but he doesn't look like a monster either. He's young, too. You wouldn't guess he was a wolf, a rapist.

He must be fucking with me. To call me again, like nothing happened. He must think I'm the kind of person you can fuck with. Maybe everyone thinks this. Maybe this is why it keeps happening.

The third time he called, I told him if he didn't stop I would call the police. Matt doesn't call anymore.

What will I do if I bump into Matt one day? What does one do when they bump into their rapist?

Thank God I'm going to Blueland. There's no Matt in Blueland.

CHAPTER 7
Blueland

The Wolf bit deep into my blue heart 'til all the happiness bled out. Mama pulled me out of the arms of the forest and stitched me back together. When people ask about the scars on my chest, I tell them a wolf tried to devour me.

When I knew what The Wolf had done to me, I phoned him. I said "Go see a doctor. Get some help."

What I really wanted to say was, "Fuck you, you filthy piece of shit! I hope your fucking dick falls off!" But it didn't come out like that.

The Wolf wasn't angry or upset or anything. He didn't even deny it. I wanted a reaction, but he wouldn't give me one. It was still a game.

Underneath The Wolf's first layer was a wolf. And underneath that layer, another wolf. And underneath that one, another. You could dig to the bone, but you wouldn't find anything other than a wolf. He couldn't be anything other than a wolf. He had a wolf brain and a wolf heart and a wolf soul. This was his core, his center.

I'm partly grateful to The Wolf. After all, he helped me discover the truth. He made me realize that life is hard and painful and tragic. Fuck the title of that film *Life Is Beautiful*. It's not. It's ugly.

People call each other crazy all the time. In every culture. They're always saying, "crazy" this and "crazy" that.

People use the word crazy too loosely. When you call a crazy person crazy, it becomes personal. When someone calls me crazy, it hurts. Even if they're just joking.

There's a craziness inside of me that comes from the illness, but there's also a craziness that comes from me. A craziness that is separate from the illness.

Yes, I'm crazy because of a chemical imbalance. But I'm also crazy because I let myself be.

When Dr. Hill said I was ill, mentally ill, I gave up. I didn't fight it. I didn't try to stop when I began to twitch or talk funny or make strange humming sounds like a radiator.

Why should I accept any responsibility when I can say "I was born a blue baby"? It's easier to blame the illness. I blame it all the time.

Mama knows all of this, but she doesn't say anything until one day she can no longer stand her daughter's twitching, humming and talking funny. She says, "Amelia sweetie, you're crazy." But she says this nicely.

There's good news: Mama says we are going to Blueland, Mama and me. And I'm not going to be completely crazy anymore. I'm only going to be half crazy. Yes, half crazy. The craziness that comes from me will be lifted. All that will be left is the craziness that comes from the illness. And being half crazy isn't all that bad. Living life half crazy is tolerable. My editor says I can still be a good writer if I'm only half crazy.

Mama's plan is to force me stop being half crazy, to put me in an environment where I can't say or do crazy things. Mama knows I'd be too embarrassed to be my fucked up morbid self in front of her Mama, her sister and her cousins. She knows I won't be able to say "I'm fucking depressed," and "I fucking want to die!" in front of them. Not like I can in front of Mama and Papa and Dr. Hill.

Papa thinks Mama's right, but we're in debt and it will cost thousands of dollars to go to Blueland.

"But we have to!" Mama says. And Papa says, "Okay" even though he knows we may go bankrupt.

For eight years Mama's done it Dr. Hill's way. Mama has stood back and watched her daughter go through all the different meds, be hospitalized, and have ECT. But now, Mama is going to do things her way. Now, Mama is behind the wheel.

Dr. Hill thinks going to Blueland is a good idea. I tell him I'm nervous about not seeing him for four weeks. I think I will die without him. Dr. Hill says everything will be all right. I can always phone him. He'll take my call even if he's with a patient.

Mama calls me Amelia Blue not only because I was born a blue baby. But also because I was born in Blueland. I'm double Blue.

My sisters were born in Blueland too. But Mama says I'm the one with the Blue heart.

Mama says Blue people are passionate and warm. We're not the butchers they portray us to be on the news. These are lies. This is propaganda. The crime rate was zero before the war.

Papa says I should be proud to be Blue. Many great writers were Blue. Papa is a hypocrite. He is half Blue but he calls himself Chinese.

Mama advises me not to talk about being Blue in interviews. She worries that if people find out I'm Blue, they'll hate me. Maybe even want to kill me. "There are a lot of crazy people out there," she says. So, I say I'm Albertan. Born and bred.

Mama doesn't want me to write about Blueland either. She thinks I shouldn't write about myself, about anything personal. All my writing should be fiction. God gave me an imagination and I should use it. People lacking talent write about themselves and people they know.

I tell Mama that writing about yourself and people you know is natural. It's better to write about something you know than what you don't. Marguerite Duras wrote about herself.

Then, Mama says if I must be truthful to disguise it a little. To change names, places, people. As much as possible. So no-one will suspect. It's not just my privacy in question; I'm invading hers and Papa's and my sisters'.

Mama's right. So, I promise her I'm going to lie a little. I will do anything for Mama. I'm also going to do it so I won't get sued.

Some people think that there are only dark people in Blueland. That's not true. There are lots of blond and red haired people with light skin.

My sisters and I aren't dark because we're dark Blue. It's the Chinese in us.

I don't tell anyone I'm part Chinese. I don't identify with that culture. Maybe it's because I'm closer to Mama than Papa. Because I'd rather be like Mama.

I have no desire to go to China. I will probably never go.

But I love *The Lover*. I read it over and over again.

In *The Lover*, Marguerite Duras falls in love with a Chinese man. This book makes me glad to be part Chinese. I feel closer to Marguerite Duras than any other writer, even Sylvia Plath.

It's safe to go to Blueland now. Now, that the war is over and the awful Wolf is dead.

I remember Blueland being very beautiful. This was before the war. I don't know what it looks like now. They say the war destroyed a lot. I haven't seen Blueland for fifteen years. Half my life.

I have many horrible memories of Blueland because of The Wolf, but Blueland is still my favourite place in the world. It is my home. It is where my heart is. Mine and Mama's. Even though The Wolf broke it. We will be forever Blue.

Mama says there's a lot of love for me in Blueland. That her Mama, her sister, and her cousins all still love me. Even though I'm not a little girl anymore.

I tell Mama I love them too. But a part of me wants to hate them because of The Wolf. It's easier to hate them. Even easier is to forget them.

My Mama's Mama is the best cook in Blueland. Mama and I always talk about the stews and pies and the chicken Mama's Mama will make for us.

I loved my Mama's Mama. She taught me to pray. She spooned me when we slept. She rubbed my skin with cream when I got sunburn.

I don't blame Mama's Mama for what happened with The Wolf. It would be wrong to blame her. You can't blame all the people that get caught in the middle. You just can't.

If anyone starts asking me questions about The Wolf, I'll just say I don't want to talk about it.

Mama says everything will be fine. Everyone will just think I'm sad he's dead. But I'm not sad. I'm glad glad glad.

Mama wants me to hide my illness. No one can know that I'm manic-depressive. I don't know what I'm going to talk about if I can't talk about my illness, my depression, and wanting to die. That's 99.9% of the content of my usual conversations. I like talking about my illness, my depression, and wanting to die.

I don't think I can go for more than half an hour without doing or saying something crazy. I don't think I can stop twitching, talking funny, making strange humming sounds.

Mama says I can smoke cigarettes in Blueland, because everyone smokes in Blueland. Mama also says I can drink half a glass of beer. She says I'll be so happy eating Blueland pies, stews, and chicken and smoking Blueland cigarettes and drinking Blueland beer. So happy I'll forget all about my depression. Mama says the blue in Blueland will heal me. But I'm worried Mama thinks that the moment I step on Blueland soil, I will immediately be normal. And happy.

Blueland is a wonderful place.

All except for the ethnic problems. You see, there are two main ethnic groups: the light Blues and the dark Blues. They hate each other. People always hate each other for being different.

Mama and Papa didn't raise us to hate. I didn't know about the ethnic problems 'til the war, when I asked Mama and Papa why they were fighting.

The light Blues wanted segregation. Canada was appalled by the war. This is hypocritical. After all, doesn't Québec want segregation too?

Mama doesn't want me to talk about my writing. She's told my relatives that I'm an editor and I write novels in my spare time. Mama wants me to be vague. If anyone asks me what I write about, I should say I write about love. Of course.

No one can know that I always use the word "fuck" and I write about having many lovers and being bisexual. If anyone in Blueland knew I had been with women, had loved women, they'd think I was strange strange strange.

There is very little homosexuality in Blueland. There is a lot of cheating, but very little homosexuality. The few gays that there are keep their sexuality in the closet. When Mama's cousin found her husband with another man it was a huge scandal. Everyone said he was "sick".

Maybe if I had lived in Blueland instead of Alberta I never would've been with women. Maybe I would've gotten married to a man when I was eighteen. Like Mama did.

It's hard enough to be a Blue manic-depressive. It's worse being a Blue bisexual manic-depressive. Or the Mama of a Blue bisexual manic-depressive.

In Blueland, people get married when they're young. In Blueland it's strange for a thirty-year-old woman not to be married. So Mama told everyone I have a boyfriend and we're probably going to get engaged soon. Mama says in a couple of years she's going to have to lie that I got married.

I decide I will lie that Matt is my boyfriend. I will show them the photo I took of Matt and me. I didn't know why I took it at the time but I have it and he's not ugly. So I might as well use it. Good thing I didn't draw devil's horns on him.

That bastard owes me this much. It's gives me a sick sadistic pleasure to use Matt like this. Mama doesn't know who Matt is. Only that he's a friend.

Matt being my boyfriend isn't the furthest thing from the truth. We had sex. And if I wanted to, I could have sex with him all the time. This is practically a boyfriend.

Mama says people lie all the time. Some lies are necessary. We need them to get by.

Mama says I'm an important person in Blueland. That people in Blueland see me as being practically an American. Practically from Hollywood. Like a movie star.

So I pretend I'm Natalie Wood. Coming from Hollywood.

I have a younger cousin who has a great body. She is my rival. She wears halter tops and miniskirts. I wear long sleeved shirts and long skirts that hide my fat.

Mama says I have to be sexier. Not a slut, but sexy. This is a lot of pressure. I can't be crazy, I can't be depressed, I have to lie about my writing, I have to lie about having a boyfriend, and on top of all this I have to be sexy. This is one tall order.

It took three fucking planes to get to Blueland. The turbulence was so bad on the first plane, I was certain Mama and I were going to die.

"At least we'll die together," Mama said. Mama always looks at the bright side of things.

I call Dr. Hill on my cell phone. I tell him that the plane is going to crash. He tells me to take a tranquilizer. So, I do.

Mama says there is going to be less turbulence on the second plane, a jumbo jet, but Mama is wrong. She has never been wrong in her entire life. And because she is wrong, I'm even more certain we're going to die.

It's an eight hour flight. And I spend most of the eight hours staring out the window into the white. I can't see mountains, valleys, forests, water, not even clouds. Just white. Mama thinks this is strange, to be staring into nothingness. I tell Mama I don't have to stop being half crazy yet. We're not in Blueland.

I call my editor and tell him I'm going to die. He tells me to finish the last chapter, to fax it to him A.S.A.P. And to take a tranquilizer. So I do.

I write some crap about a woman meeting her doppelganger and exchanging souls with her. I put my writing in the plastic bag the airline magazine came in. So it doesn't get wet if we end up in the ocean.

When we miraculously survive this flight, I search the airport for a fax machine. I can't find one. But I find a McDonalds.

Mama assures me that the last flight will be smooth, because it's a Blueland plane with Blueland pilots. Mama is wrong again. This flight is the most horrific of them all.

Mama doesn't look like Mama anymore. The hair and make-up are the same, but Mama doesn't look the same. I'm frightened because Mama doesn't look the same. I wonder if I'm sitting next to Mama's doppelganger. I'm caught between life and fiction.

I begin to cry. But I'm not crying because we might nose dive fifty or twenty thousand or whatever feet down. I'm crying because we had such shitty lives. Because we are poor. Because I was always ill. And, of course, because of The Wolf.

Mama tells me take a tranquilizer. So, I do.

This is a three hour flight and when I'm not writing I'm eating cheese and staring at the attractive male flight attendant's ass. Mama lets me eat her cheese too. She calls me her "little mouse".

In two hours, Mama has grown stranger, almost unrecognizable. Then it dawns on me that it would take something as stupendous as a plane crash to tear the cord between Mama and me.

I wish I could have one last fuck. I'd like it to be with the attractive male flight attendant, but he's probably gay. But maybe he's thinking what I'm thinking: that this plane is going down and we're going to be eaten by a giant octopus. Maybe it wouldn't make any difference whose fist is up his ass. Maybe I could persuade him to go into the cramped bathroom with me and relieve some tension.

I wonder what they'll say on the news. Will Mama and I just be "two Canadians" or will we be "author Amelia Blue and her mother"?

I ask the male flight attendant if this much turbulence is unusual. He tells me to take a tranquilizer. So, I do.

When we get to Blueland, I exhale. Mama looks like herself again. But I look a little blue.

When my uncle picks Mama and me up from the airport, he is in a good mood. He looks like how I remember him except his hair is grayer. I wonder why he doesn't dye it.

There's pop, chocolate, and candy in the back seat of his car. It's like I'm still fourteen, but I say "Thank you".

My uncle is a liar and a gambler and a thief. I heard a story about him putting a pair of running shoes and walking out of the store without paying for them.

During this six hour drive, my uncle persuades Mama to participate in a scheme he has concocted. My uncle is a funny guy. We always said he could be a comedian. So, when he tells us we should blackmail my dead Mama's Papa's mistress, we think he's only half serious.

My uncle says he was informed that my Mama's Papa paid for his mistress's house and bought all the furniture. My uncle is a liar and a gambler and a thief but he is well informed. I know, because my Mama's Papa told me he had paid for the house and bought the furniture.

My Mama's Papa liked to boast. When he was drunk he'd say "I have two women." Mama says there were even more. Mama says there were rumours that he was sleeping with her teachers. It was written on the school's bathroom walls.

My Mama's Papa lived with his wife but he saw his mistress on the side for thirty five years. Everyone knew.

He introduced me to his mistress when I was eight. I remember thinking she wasn't very pretty. But she was nice. She had her own store and let me have as much candy as I wanted. I didn't say "You slut! You horrible woman!" I was only eight.

A man can cause so much pain, can make so many people miserable. And yet when he dies, be forgiven for everything. The truth becomes distorted. The story changes. He was "good, decent, and generous," they say.

My Mama's Papa took me to see his mistress several times. My Mama's Mama would hear from her sources that I had been there. She would cry and ask me if I had kissed her. I said, "No". But I had given her a quick kiss on the cheek.

I felt sorry for Mama's Mama. That her husband was cheating on her. But in Blueland all the men were cheating on their wives. That's just the way it was.

My uncle thinks that since my Mama's Papa's mistress has no children, she should leave her house and furniture to her lover's children. Mama and her sister were the closest thing to being her own. If she doesn't leave the house and furniture to them, they should forbid the mistress to continue to visit their father's grave.

My uncle is sly. He says Mama and her sister deserve this after all the grief "the whore" had caused them. That "the whore" should pay. That my Mama's Papa should've spent his money on his daughters instead of a whore.

My uncle says Mama and her sister will take care of her funeral, her grave, her tombstone, and the flowers. Like real daughters. If the mistress puts them in her will.

My uncle says he's willing to do just about anything for his wife to get half the house and furniture. He will phone the mistress, visit her, bring her food, bring her medication. He says he'll even fuck her if he has to. This is very funny to Mama and me.

Then my uncle says, we can bury my Mama's Mama beside my Mama's Papa and his mistress on top of him. Mama and I are peeing ourselves laughing. What a joker he is.

Later, when the idea to blackmail the mistress comes up, my uncle makes it look like Mama thought of the whole thing by herself.

I tell Mama's sister I heard everything. That it was the other way around. It was her husband's fucking idea. He was trying to hook Mama in. But Mama's sister believes the man she's been married to for twenty years.

We were supposed to spend most of the four weeks in the village at my Mama's Mama's. I was supposed to eat pies and stews and chicken and fresh tomatoes from my Mama's Mama's garden. I was supposed to sip espressos on the patio. I was supposed to drink water from the well.

When Mama saw her Mama she didn't cry because it had been fifteen years. She cried because her Mama looked so thin. "Like death", Mama said to me later.

When Mama's Mama and I are alone, we talk about her garden and her infected toe. I tell her she should go to the doctor. But she says she'll wait.

Then, she talks about her dead husband, how she stayed with him even though he had a mistress. How other women would've left. How people think she's a brave woman.

Then, we talk about Manuel. How he was so handsome, charming, and clever.

When Mama's Mama starts talking about The Wolf, I try to change the subject. She persists. She wants to know about the phone conversation. She says The Wolf was distraught. That he collapsed. I'm glad to hear this.

I could tell her all about the big bad wolf. But he's dead. He's not going to rise from the dead. I've won.

I say I don't want to talk any more and walk away. I don't want to be alone with Mama's Mama any more.

Mama, her Mama, and her sister had to go to court because of the land they inherited when my Mama's Papa died. It was to be split into three equal sections between them. And when Mama's Mama died her third was supposed to be split in half between Mama and Mama's sister.

Mama's sister said she didn't want to split the house. She wanted the entire house. She felt she deserved it because she was the one who took care of my Mama's Papa's funeral, grave, and tombstone. Even though Mama paid for most of it.

Mama asks her Mama for some flowers from her garden to put on her Papa's and Manuel's graves. Mama's Mama refuses. We don't know why. This is the first sign that something is wrong with Mama's Mama.

We postpone going to the cemetery.

Mama's aunt says when my Mama's Papa died, my Mama's Mama was lost. She was too used to her life with him, her life of servitude. She did everything for him. She made his dinner, washed and ironed his clothes, and cleaned up after him, like Mama does for me. This was her purpose in life. When her husband died, she lost her purpose, her life became meaningless.

My Mama's Mama's eyes were dark. Black one would say. There was no depth. Only surface. Like Buddy's.

Now, Mama's Mama's eyes are blue. Clear blue. I didn't know a person's eye color could change with age. I wonder if it's from the diabetes.

Now, I can peer into them. But I see nothing. There is nothing inside of her. She died along with her husband. If you dig up his grave, you'll find her lying next to him.

It was very hot. Mama and I were sweaty. We washed every day. Mama's Mama didn't like this. She said it was unholy to wash on Sundays. She said we were using up all her water. Her water.

People in Blueland don't have shower curtains. When I ask Mama why they don't have shower curtains Mama says it's because they don't have shower rods.

Anyway, since there were no shower curtains it was very difficult not to get the floor wet. I was extra careful, but there may have been a drop or two. Mama's Mama said there was water everywhere, that we had left a terrible mess. We were dirty, and her bathroom smelled like vomit.

I thought Mama's Mama was senile or something. Maybe she had killed too many chickens. Chopping off a hundred heads is going to affect you sooner or later.

On the third day, after arguing some more with Mama, Mama's sister asked my uncle to drive her home. They left Mama and me alone with Mama's Mama.

Mama's Mama said terrible things. Like Mama and I were evil, that we were witches. We should go to church and pray for our tainted souls. She said that I had killed The Wolf, shortened his life by at least five years and that if I was worth anything I would've been married by now. She said no one wanted me.

Then the phone rang and Mama's Mama got the news that her brother was in the hospital. I told her God was punishing her.

I thought Mama's Mama was going to strangle Mama or me. Or that one of us was going to have a fucking heart attack. So Mama and I packed our suitcases and left. Before someone died.

Mama's Mama had driven us out. After three days, she had driven us out.

Mama's Mama returned all the money, over a thousand dollars, and all the presents we brought her. "Take your rags!" she said of the dresses we gave her.

She didn't return the medication we brought her for her infected toe. This she kept.

The next day, Mama's sister phoned us at Manuel's. She blamed Mama and me for everything. She said we shouldn't have upset her Mama. That she was a sick old woman. She could have another stroke. We could've killed her. And why did we go to Manuel's? Mama's sister didn't like Manuel's widow. She thought Theresa wore too much make-up.

Mama's sister says we should've called her, gone to her house. I point out to Mama's sister that she was the one who left us. There was no way we were going to stay with her husband, who was the cause of our arguing.

Mama's sister made it sound like we had attacked Mama's Mama, cornered her. It was two against one. She was a victim.This was the story Mama's Mama had told Mama's sister and Mama's sister would tell Mama's cousins and anyone else who was interested. Thank God, everyone was on mine and Mama's side.

I may never see my Mama's Mama and my Mama's sister ever again. I probably won't even put flowers on their graves. Or maybe I will. Because I'm Blue, and the Blue forgive their dead.

Maybe the flowers will be blue.

Theresa and her son, Eddie, took us in. We joked that we were refugees.

Thank God they rescued us. Otherwise, we would have had to stay with Papa's depressed family.

Dear reader, it's not like I hate Papa's family. They're not crazy or immoral or perverted. But their depression will smother you. You won't be able to have a proper bowel movement.

Maybe I would have gone if I knew they had a scale and shower curtains.

In Blueland you have to pay to use a public washroom. People kiss each other when they meet. Everyone smokes cigarettes and drinks alcohol. There's no diet cola and no low-fat muffins. Yet, no-one is fat. I saw, like, two fat ladies. They were in their sixties.

They don't have scales either. I asked Mama how people knew if they gained weight. Mama said they can tell by how their clothes fit. This isn't good enough for me. I need fucking numbers.

I weigh myself every day. How was I going to survive four weeks without a scale? Mama should've told me.

One of my cousins gained twenty pounds on her holiday. I am completely convinced I will gain twenty pounds too. I'm going to gain a pound every day.

Whenever we go to someone's house I immediately go to the bathroom to search for a scale.

I ask Eddie and Theresa every day if I have gained weight. Theresa says an attractive girl like me shouldn't worry so much about gaining weight.

Eddie says "Eat what you want." Then he squeezes half an inch of fat on his stomach. "See how fat I am?" Eddie is as thin as a Chinaman.

I stop going out. I didn't want to leave Manuel's apartment. If I saw those skinny women with their skinny legs and skinny asses I would get depressed, suicidal. Never had I felt fatter in my entire life.

One day, one of my Mama's rail thin cousins said I should do some exercises to tone my thighs. That was it. I had reached my limit. I went to the balcony and threatened to jump.

Mama talked me out of it. She said her cousin was crazy, that she said crazy things all the time. That she was jealous because she couldn't put on weight, be more womanly, voluptuous. That I shouldn't kill myself because of a woman who brought us grapes with spiders all over them.

I call Dr. Hill and tell him I want to kill myself because I'm fat. He says it's probably just water retention.

I decide to wait 'til we return to Alberta to kill myself. I don't want to embarrass Mama in Blueland with my suicide. I owe her this much.

After this scene, Mama gave up on her dream for her daughter to be only half crazy.

Poor Mama. Her brother is dead. Her father is dead. Now she has lost her Mama and her only sister. And then there's me.

The tombstone Mama had spent so much money on was lovely. Manuel deserved it.

Mama and I cry and cry. It's like Manuel's death all over again.

Manuel's widow, Theresa, and his son, Edward, are not crying. Mama and I are startled at their coolness. Perhaps Theresa and Edward have cried so many tears, they have no more to shed.

As for me, I'm humming like a radiator. Theresa and Edward are looking at me. This time, I try to stop humming. It takes a few attempts, but I succeed. Theresa and Edward are no longer looking at me.

It is in this moment of mourning that I find strength and hope. I realize that I can be only half crazy someday.

There is one problem. Manuel was supposed to be buried in the Catholic part of the cemetery. Somehow, he ended up with the atheists. This upset Mama greatly. No one had told her.

The Wolf's tombstone is lovely too, but he doesn't deserve it.

He looks thin in his picture. Mama says he was thin when he died. It's hard to imagine The Wolf anything but fat.

I feel powerful standing over The Wolf's grave. I feel I have conquered him by outliving him. What Mama has been telling me all along, Mama's words resonate in my head, "He's dead and you're alive."

I feel like spitting on his grave. I feel like ripping his flowers, the flowers Mama's Mama laid on his grave that morning.

Suddenly, a crazy impulse comes over me. I want to urinate on The Wolf's grave. He had asked me to urinate on him before and I had said no. Now I am willing to give him what he wants.

I'm laughing. Not only are Theresa and Edward looking at me but Mama too. I try to stop. I try several times, but I can't. And because I can't, I have lost hope that someday I can be only half crazy.

Mama gives me a tranquilizer.

Mama's Mama was so lost. She had lost her husband. Then herself. Then Mama and me.

I felt sorry for her. Only a lost woman would do what she did. After not seeing her child and grandchild for fifteen years.

Mama's Mama hated her husband. She cursed him all the time. When my Mama's Papa tried to embrace her, she called him a fool and pushed him away.

Now that he was dead, she was the perfect wife. Bringing him flowers every Sunday. Lighting candles for him. Praying for him.

And she never spoke badly of him. No, she praised him. And, people said, sometimes she cried.

I just kept telling myself that Mama's Mama was old. She had lost her husband. She was a senile old widow.

What happened to the woman who would get up in the middle of the night to bring me water? Had this woman died with her husband? Had old age taken her? How sad it was that she was gone. I missed her.

What could I say to Mama besides, "Your Mama is a bitch"? There was nothing I could do to make her feel better. I could kill myself and make her feel worse.

I have three coffees everyday with Theresa. During coffee, I always smoke. Combining the smoking I do when I'm with Theresa and the smoking I do when I'm with Eddie, I'm turning into quite the smoker. Hopefully, I won't get addicted. I know that Mama expects me to stop when we leave Blueland. This is only a holiday luxury.

Edward, Eddie I call him, isn't tall like his dead father. He is blond and small like his Mama. We are almost the same height. Everyone thinks he didn't grow because of childhood trauma.

His skin is soft and he has a beautiful complexion. When I ask him if he had acne as an adolescent, he says, "No."

Later, he tell me he's been sexually active from a young age. "Twelve," he says. I've heard that young men who are sexually active have better complexions than those who wait.

Mama says Eddie looks like Manuel from behind. She says they have the same back of the head and shoulders, and he walks like Manuel. Mama says Eddie is a miniature version of his father. I don't see it. I just don't see it. I keep asking him to turn around. I stare but I don't see Manuel in him. I only see Theresa.

I remember Eddie as a child. He was five the last time I saw him.

He was so clever. He knew all these dirty jokes. Everyone thought it was so amusing to listen to him talk about penises and vaginas. No one said it was inappropriate, but Theresa would act embarrassed and tell him to shut up. He'd just tell her to shut up back. Theresa seemed more like his sister than his Mama.

After Manuel died, Eddie became the man of the house. He smoke and drank in excess. To prove his manhood, I think. He called his Mama by her first name.

Besides being sexually active, he's been driving since he was twelve. Manuel taught him before he died. Eddie is a good driver when he's not intoxicated.

One night he was caught by the police. He had had thirteen or fourteen drinks. Blueland beer is far more potent than Canadian beer.

I was the only one bold enough or crazy enough to tell Eddie he was going to kill someone or die in a car crash just like his father. But he just said, "Whatever is meant to happen, will happen."

Instead of scolding him, Mama gave him a hundred dollars to pay the fine.

Mama says he'll have to enlist in the army soon. Then he'll be more serious, mature. He'll get a job and get married. Then, it'll all be different.

Young men get in trouble, Mama says. That's the way young men are. They drink and smoke and get into trouble. It'll pass.

I want to shake Eddie, shake some sense into him. He's given up just like I have. For me it was when the doctor said I was mentally ill. For Eddie, it was when his father died.

Poor Eddie. When they told him his father wasn't coming home, ever, Eddie found his father's gun and was about to blow his brains out. The Wolf caught him just in time.

How can we not feel sorry for him? How many twelve-year-olds do you know that have put a loaded gun in their mouth? Pain like that stays with you forever.

And it wasn't just that it was Eddie's father. It was Manuel. No-one on earth was as handsome and clever and as wonderful as Manuel. No-one. We all knew it.

Mama's sister was the only one Mama told about The Wolf. Now Mama is so broken she tells Theresa and Eddie. Thank God they believe Mama. They say The Wolf was a pig. They hope he is burning in hell.

I was glad they knew. I felt freed. Because of this freedom, I no longer felt embarrassed to say or do crazy things in front of Eddie and Theresa. This is the price of freedom, dear reader.

I began to twitch and talk funny and hum. I didn't even try to stop.

The Mama's Mama I loved, the Mama's Mama that brought me water in the middle of the night, was dead.

This replacement, this wrack of bones, who complained her bathroom wasn't clean anymore, wasn't my Mama's Mama. Perhaps it was her doppelganger. That there were two Mama's Mama's. One was dead. And the other wreaking havoc in Blueland.

But Mama says Mama's Mama didn't hug her, wasn't affectionate with her even when she was a child. That there were glimpses of this Mama's Mama, the Mama's Mama that drove us away.

I knew The Wolf was inside me, Mama, my aunt, and my sisters. But I didn't think he was inside her. She had different blood. But he possessed her. She looked like my Mama's Mama, but she was him.

Mama's Mama had a bad life. Her husband was her boss, he cheated on her, she lost her precious son. I couldn't hate her. Had she had a better life, maybe I could.

When I was a kid, I wanted to be like Mama's sister. To be tall and thin like her. To smoke cigarettes like her. My Mama's sister and I have exactly the same hands.

Mama phoned her sister every day to beg her to stop smoking. She spent thousands of dollars telling her to stop. This is what a good sister does.

What had Mama's sister turned into? Her father, The Wolf, her husband, all three? Maybe she became them and lost herself. She replaced herself with these men, but her hands remained the same.

The poison, the evil had seeped into her heart. Her heart was as black as her lungs were from twenty years of chain smoking.

Why did Mama's sister betray Mama like that? If it was for the money, then she was a fool because she could've gotten a lot more out of her had she not fucked everything up. The only conclusion Mama and I could come to was that she did it because of The Wolf. She hated me and Mama because Mama had told her what The Wolf had done to me.

Over beer and cigarettes, I tell Eddie about the kitten, and the hen, and The Wolf asking me to pee in his mouth. I notice I hadn't shed a tear. Maybe it wasn't so odd that Eddie and Theresa didn't cry at Manuel's grave.

To bring me some comfort, Eddie tells me that The Wolf suffered terribly before he died. He knows he suffered because he visited him in the hospital. This information does give me pleasure. Eddie says The Wolf was writhing in pain.

I want to tell Eddie everything. Like a guilty Catholic wants to tell a priest his sins. I want to tell him about being with women, about Matt, about my illness. When he gently strokes my hand, I want to fall asleep like a baby. I want to sleep in his arms because he soothes me.

When I saw a picture of him last year, he seemed so effeminate I thought he might be gay. He isn't. Eddie loves women, just like his father did. I think when Eddie gets married, he'll still have women on the side.

Somehow, Manuel and Eddie being womanizers doesn't bother me like my Mama's Papa being a womanizer. It amuses me. Like Eddie telling those dirty little jokes when he was five.

I find myself staring at Eddie, at the back of his head, his shoulders, how he walks. Maybe he is like Manuel. Maybe I was mistaken. Maybe I was blind. I see now how one can be blind to things, not see what is obvious, what is right in front of them.

Manuel may have been the perfect male specimen, but Eddie was the perfect combination of male and female. He was like a gay man who wasn't gay. Poor Eddie must get hit on by a lot of men. I don't ask him about this. I don't want to embarrass him.

At first, I thought Eddie would have to get a girl liquored up to get her into bed. Now I see how irresistible Eddie is. With his soft skin, his beautiful complexion, and his boyish charm.

We brought three suitcases of clothes for Mama's sister, her husband and their son. Later, Mama's sister said we couldn't buy her love.

If money didn't matter to her, why did she want the house and the land so badly? Surely not for sentimental reasons. Mama's sister was not sentimental like Mama.

We wondered if her husband had talked her into it. Perhaps blackmailed her. Or maybe even beat her. But there were no bruises.

I had always thought that even though Mama's Mama didn't have much schooling and was from the village, that she was very intelligent. But after Mama's Mama drove us out, all I could think was, "What a stupid woman! What a stupid woman!"

What did I do to her? Was she still mad I had gone to see my Mama's Papa's mistress? Was she mad because I didn't write? If she were mad because of the mistress and me not writing, I could understand. But maybe Mama is right, maybe Mama's Mama is mad at me because of the phone call I made, because of what I had said to The Wolf.

Mama's Mama continued to tell people how dirty Mama and I were and complained how often we showered to everyone. If we were so fucking dirty, she should be glad we were showering.

She disowned Mama. She signed over her third entirely to Mama's sister. Which meant Mama's sister would get two thirds and Mama would only get one third.

This was a huge blow to Mama. It was bad enough Mama's Mama had sold Manuel's land to her brothers. Now she was taking away what her father had meant for her to have.

Mama was going to let her sister and her husband, the thief, have everything. I told Mama to claim her third out of principal. To be a thorn in their side.

This time I was the one who saw the bright side of things. I told Mama if she was going to get a third of the house to claim the bathroom for hers. Then we could decide how much showering was going on. We would control the water.

My Mama's sister could've not accepted Mama's Mama's third. She should've refused what rightfully belonged to her older sister.

Shit! It just occurred to me that I might be buried in the same cemetery as The Wolf and my Mama's Mama! Death is not the end all people think it is. Some things you can never escape.

Mama's cousins tried to mend things between Mama and Mama's sister. They all went out for a drink and talked, but the alcohol wouldn't penetrate Mama's sister's stone heart.

After everything was said and done, Mama and I came to the conclusion that Mama's sister and her fucking husband had planned it like this all along. They wanted Mama's Mama to quarrel with us so she would sign over her third to them. This is why they left us alone on the third day. Dear reader, it was all about the money. There was no love there.

Mama's sister made several phone calls but none of them seemed like earnest attempts to resolve things. I think she just wanted to aggravate us further.

In the end, she said it was my all my fault. I knew what she was actually blaming me for. I told Mama if she called again, I would threaten to go to the newspapers about The Wolf. She didn't call.

The last time I saw Mama's sister was in court. She didn't say anything to me. She didn't even wave at me. But she was wearing the shoes and the necklace I had given her. She didn't return the clothes and the money like Mama's Mama did.

Mama wanted to have a relationship with her sister's son, Adam. She loved him. She wanted to be in his life. She wanted to be a good aunt. She'd give him presents, money, whatever he wanted. He never asked for anything, which made us love him even more.

He smoked behind his parents' backs. And kept his girlfriends secret. But that's about it.

He is a very smart boy. He can speak English fluently. He taught himself.

Mama's sister and her husband bought him a computer to keep him out of trouble. If everything hadn't turned to shit, we could've e-mailed each other.

The last time I saw him, was when Mama's cousins were trying to reconcile Mama and Mama's sister. They went out for a drink while Eddie, Adam and I watched

The Time Machine (another Jeremy Irons film). My favourite line is "You are the inescapable result of your tragedy."

I said, "Our vacation is ruined." All my cousin said was, "No comment."

He was going to get two thirds of the house and the land while my sisters and I were only going to get one third. I bet if I asked him if this was fair, he'd say "No comment" again.

Someday, we could've shared our grandparents's house and land. We should have lived harmoniously. Now we are destined to be enemies.

He is on his parents' side. They brainwashed him. I knew this by his "No comment".

Mama was going to still send him money for every birthday. I told Mama she was a fool.

When Mama and I are in Blueland we have lunch with my Mama's Papa's mistress. The mistress had phoned and asked. Otherwise, we wouldn't have gone.

How strange it must be for Mama. Her Mama hates this woman. This woman caused her and her Mama so many problems. So much grief, humiliation, and embarrassment.

Mama's father is dead, but she still feels obligated to see his mistress. Only in Mama's and my fucked up lives is a mistress like family.

I have no love for this woman, but a part of me feels sorry for her. Like I feel sorry for Monica Lewinsky.

People have called her a whore and a home breaker. They blamed her. Not my Mama's Papa. Why do people always blame the woman? It's not fair.

My Mama's Papa had many lovers. No one called him a whore. Same with The Wolf. Why are only women called "whores" in the straight world?

After Zowie, I no longer know what a whore is. Are you a whore when you sleep with twenty people, ten people, five people? What is the definition of a whore? Who decides?

I had many lovers. Maybe people think I'm whore. Mama says I'm different. I was sick.

When we see the mistress, we are shocked. Not as shocked as when we saw Mama's Mama, but shocked. The mistress looks terrible. Her red hair is half gray.

She is too thin. She has completely let herself go. The mistress and Mama are almost the same age, but the mistress looks old enough to be Mama's Mama.

Mama tells her she should gain some weight and dye her hair. Some women would say nothing. Mama is nice.

The mistress talks about how she loved my Mama's Papa. How she wished she had had children with him. How she's thinking about killing herself with a bomb while holding a picture of him.

She's crying, but none of this moves me. It sounds like bullshit. It makes me sick to listen to her. I want to vomit my lunch.

Inside, I'm thinking, "Fuck you!" Not "Fuck you, you whore!" But "Fuck you!" But I'm smiling, speaking softly to her, holding her hand.

As for Mama, she's looking the mistress in the eye. But I can tell Mama's somewhere else.

Lunch is supposed to be an hour long, but it turns into two. I give Mama a look that says "Let's go. I've reached my limit."

So Mama says we have to go, and the mistress says "All right." We give her a hug and a kiss on each cheek.

The mistress wants to pay for lunch, but Mama won't let her. Mama pays.

We stayed at Manuel's for four weeks. Theresa even let us sleep in Manuel's bed, which was the most comfortable bed I'd ever slept in. Even better than my orthopedic mattress. During the day, Mama's sister's and my Mama's Mama's treatment of us ate away at me. At night, I slept like a baby. Better than I'd ever slept in my entire life.

Eddie let us watch the video of Manuel's funeral.

To my surprise, Manuel looks the same in death as in life. He looks like a movie star. I haven't been to many funerals, but Manuel was by far the loveliest corpse I'd ever seen and probably will ever see. He doesn't look dead. He looks asleep. And he's almost smiling. I don't feel bad anymore because he seems happy.

I've seen photographs of Papa's dead sister and dead uncle. They looked horrible, frightening. I had nightmares.

My aunt kisses Manuel's face at the funeral. This doesn't repulse me. He looks so beautiful. I tell Mama I would kiss him too. It would be nice to kiss him. Like kissing Jesus. Mama says she would kiss Manuel too.

Mama and I cry while we're watching this video. Theresa isn't howling. She is quiet. Eddie is too.

Eddie is trying to look strong in front of Mama and me. Because he is the man of the house. But Theresa, I don't understand. She is a lock no key fits into.

I remember an old woman who went to the cemetery every day, and cried at the top of her lungs. Like a shrieking sound. Everyone knew about her. She had lost her young daughter twenty years ago. She's been crying like this, at the top of her lungs, for twenty years.

This shrieking will haunt me forever, haunt everyone in Blueland. Someone where in the back of my mind, this old woman will be shrieking.

I could see Mama ending up like this woman if I died, if I killed myself. She would go to the cemetery and cry at the top of her lungs every day. She would never get over my death, my suicide. Maybe she would go crazy.

Every now and then, when I want to kill myself, I think of this poor woman crying, shrieking. And it stops me from ruining Mama's life.

In Blueland, people are always cleaning the tombstones, cutting the grass, bringing fresh flowers and lighting candles for their dead. In Blueland, people are obsessed with the dead and death. But it's not strange or creepy. It's beautiful and romantic. Maybe this is why I want to die. Maybe if I weren't Blue, I wouldn't want to die so much. Had I come from a land where death was scary and awful, maybe I wouldn't be so suicidal.

In Blueland, when someone dies, no one speaks badly of them ever again. Their flaws are forgotten and their sins forgiven. They are in heaven now. This part I don't like, don't agree with. There's no way The Wolf was going to heaven. No fucking way!

Dr. Hill says that we each perceive things differently. We each have a separate reality. My truth is not your truth, and your truth is not mine.

My reality of The Wolf is different because he molested me. If he hadn't, I would remember him as a wonderful man. Even though he had a mistress, drank too much, sometimes beat his wife.

I try to forget The Wolf. Try to pretend he never existed.

We are celebrating Mama's sister's birthday. Eating cake outside, under the grape vine. Erase The Wolf. No Wolf.

We are roasting corn over an open fire. Erase The Wolf. No Wolf.

We are in the house, watching a Natalie Wood film on T.V. Erase The Wolf. No Wolf.

There. Brand new memories. The old ones altered, recycled. I have recycled memories.

When Mama and I come home, Papa doesn't yell at us because of the money. He tells us he had our dog put to sleep. His hips gave out and he couldn't walk anymore and it was the humane thing to do.

Mama cried that night. I wish I could've given her a reason to be happy. I wish I could've been only half crazy for her. But I'm ready to go to the vet and pay him a hundred and fifty dollars to put me down too.

I realize if I wasn't depressed and didn't want to die, I wouldn't be Amelia Blue. I'd be someone else.

If you dig inside me, underneath the depression there's more depression. And underneath that, even more. Like a box inside a box inside a box. No surprise. No prize. Just another empty fucking box.

Chapter 8

Me

I'm fucked. Totally fucked.
I'm sitting in our tub. Staring at our orange scale.
I'm trembling. I'm not cold. I have my clothes on. There's no water.
I'm trembling because I'm scared. Scared to step on the orange scale.
Mama knocks.
"What is my Amelia Blue doing?"
"Nothing, Mama."
Mama will think I'm crazy. Totally crazy. Totally fucked.
This orange scale knows the truth. I'm afraid of the truth. Afraid of this orange scale.
"You've been in there forever, Amelia Blue."
"I have a stomach ache, Mama."
Fucking fat. I want to get rid of this fat. I want to cut it off. Off my arms, my thighs, my ass. I should just cut this fat off with a pair of scissors.
I want to be a fish. I want fins and scales and I want a tail.
"Do you want some orange soda?"
"Mama, leave me the fuck alone!"
Maybe I can weigh one toe. Then, another.
Fuck it!
I can't fucking do it!
I'm fucked!
Totally fucked!

   Dr. H: How was your trip?
A: I'm fat.
   Dr. H: Was the weather nice?
A: I'm fat.
   Dr. H: You have a nice tan.
A: I'm fucking fat!
   Dr. H: Did you weigh yourself?
A: No.
   Dr. H: Why not?
A: Never mind.

Dr. H: You don't look like you've gained weight.

A: You're just saying that so I don't kill myself.

Dr. H: No, I'm not.

A: Yes.

Dr. H: Maybe you should weigh yourself.

A: I don't fucking want to. Okay?

Dr. H: Your Mama told me what happened with her Mama and sister.

A: I hope they have diarrhea for the rest of their lives.

Dr. H: It's all right to be angry.

A: That fucking Wolf. That fucking prick. He fucking ruined my fucking life. And he's still fucking ruining it.

Dr. H: He's dead, Amelia.

A: I'm so fucking fat. I disgust myself. No wonder no one loves me.

Dr. H: Lots of people love you.

A: Like who?

Dr. H: Your Mama.

A: Besides her.

Dr. H: Your Papa.

A: Besides him.

Dr. H: Well, there's…

A: No-one! X didn't love me! Francis didn't love me! Buddy didn't love me! Vincent didn't love me!

Dr. H: Vincent was a jerk. He deceived you.

A: I'm going to fucking kill myself.

Dr. H: Do you want a tranquilizer?

A: That's all you do is give me drugs. You're turning me into a drug addict. I'm going to O.D.

Dr H: Do you feel you're being overmedicated?

A: No. I'm going to kill myself. How are you going to feel when I'm dead?

Dr. H: I would be very sad. I'd miss you.

A: No you wouldn't.

Dr. H: You know that if I think you're a danger to yourself, I'll have to hospitalize you.

A: Please don't. I'll be good.
    Dr H: Are you sure?
A: Yes…no…yes.
    Dr. H: Okay. See you next week?
A: Can I have a hug?
    Dr. H: Sure.
A: Can I have a tranquilizer?
    Dr. H: Of course.

Something is wrong with our tap water. It tastes funny. I think it's contaminated. I'm not going to drink tap water anymore.

I tell Mama and Papa not to drink it either. But they don't listen. They ignore me.

There's probably hexavalent chromium or whatever in our water. We're probably going to get cancer.

We should sue someone. I should call Erin Brokovich.

Maybe if I get cancer, I will be skinny. Maybe I will die.

I have to finish this book. I'll drink bottled water until I'm finished.

I buy thirty bottles of mineral water imported from Blueland. Blueland mineral water is the safest.

When Mama sees thirty bottles of mineral water in my room, she thinks it's strange.

I notice that the caps are a little loose. What if someone hasopened the bottles? What if someone spat in them because they hate Blue people? They think we're fascists.

I call the store and tell the manager that the caps are loose, but he won't give me a refund.

Mama told me a story about the king of Blueland. When he was afraid someone was going to poison his water, he had it put in a tank with fish. If the fish didn't die, the water was safe to drink.

So I go to the pet store where I bought the crickets. I buy a 130 gallon tank and one orange goldfish. This costs me $500.75 When Mama finds out, she is upset.

I empty all thirty bottles into the tank, but it's hardly enough. So, I add tap water. And pray.

I name my fish David Bowie. Mama says she never heard of a fish with a first name and a last name. She says I should just call him Bowie.

Mama also says that 130 gallons is a lot for one fish. I tell her David Bowie is claustrophobic.

Mama calls Dr. Hill. Dr. Hill prescribes more meds.

My dream has changed. No more tall men in tall houses.

Now I'm driving a car.

In the back seat, there's a dead body. This dead body looks like me. There are two of me.

A police car is following us.

Which one is the real me?

Did I kill the other one?

Dr. Hill says dreams are just electrical impulses firing in our brain at random.

I stare at David Bowie for hours. Is this strange?

Mama thinks it's strange. But is it any stranger than staring at a T.V.?

David Bowie isn't happy.

I'm worried David Bowie is sick. I ask him. If he swims to the right it's "yes" and if he swims to the left it's "no". David Bowie says he's not sick.

I ask him if he's lonely. He answers yes. I decide to get him a companion. After all, fish need love too.

I go to the pet store and buy another goldfish. This one has a black stripe. I name her Amelia Blue.

Mama says she's afraid that if the fish dies, I will die too.

I'm sitting in a seedy bar, writing. Sabrina comes in. I haven't seen her since we went to Calgary with Buddy.

She looks the same: black hair, black clothes, heavy black make-up. She's pretty in a Marilyn Manson sort of way.

I pretend to not notice her, but she sees me and comes over.

"So you're a writer now, Mel" she says.

She sits down. We drink whiskey. Whiskey goes very well with the new meds Dr. Hill has prescribed.

Sabrina tells me how she's been traveling through Europe and about her drug addict boyfriend.

On my fourth whiskey, we start laughing about the trip to Calgary. About how I urinated on X's mother's doorstep, about the sexy Italian baker, and all those shoes Buddy brought along.

"He probably masturbated with them," she says.

We are laughing so loud we get asked to leave. Sabrina is living in a cheap motel down the street. We go to her room. We lie on the bed, drink and eat almost everything in the mini bar and watch porn.

I tell Sabrina about my dream. Sabrina kisses me. I kiss her back.

Then, I start crying. Maybe because Buddy is dead. Maybe because I was raped. Or because my Mama's Mama and Mama's sister hate me.

Sabrina takes my pants off and goes down on me. I fall asleep.

When I awake, I check my body for cuts, in case Sabrina might've taken some blood from me while I slept.

I am quiet. So Sabrina doesn't hear me get up. I could leave then, but I don't. Instead, I sit on the corner of the bed and watch Sabrina sleep. I haven't done this since I was with Buddy.

Sabrina is a lot prettier than I realized. She shouldn't wear so much black make-up.

So, I'm walking down the street thinking "Oh God what have I done?" Am I a lesbian? I mean there was X. Then, Zowie. But Sabrina too?

One girl can be due to insanity. Two to experimentation. How do I explain three?

I know: alcohol. I was drunk and Sabrina seduced me. Yup, that's what happened. That's my story.

I go see a movie.

Other than the woman at the mall with bumps all over her skin, I compare myself to the crippled boy who works at the movie theatre.

Mama says it's worse to be crippled than depressed, but sometimes when I see him smiling in his special chair, I want to be him.

But then Mama ruins it for me. She says that maybe he hides his suffering. Maybe he's depressed too, on top of being crippled. Depressed because he's different from other people, and maybe girls don't want to date him.

I sit down by a man. There are hardly any people in the theatre. No one in my row except this man who's probably fifty. He has gray hair. And he looks pretty average. He's not hideous or fat.

The film is called *Solaris*. It takes place in the future. A psychologist is sent to a space station to find out what has happened to the crew. He ends up being visited by his dead wife who had killed herself because of depression. I am deeply moved by this movie. In fact, I love it.

I'm still disturbed by my lesbian affair. To prove to myself I'm still heterosexual, I put my hand on the crotch of the man beside me. He doesn't seem to mind, so I go further. I jerk him off. It only takes him five minutes to come.

When I'm finished, I move to the back of the theatre and finish watching the film. I don't usually stay for credits, but they are in such a unique font, I can't resist.

The man I had just given a hand job to walks by and utters two words to me. These two words are "Thank you."

It comforts me that this man is polite. It makes the experience less creepy.

Maybe I should've given this man my phone number. Maybe this man would say "Thank you" after every kiss, every blowjob, every fuck. I should be with a man like this.

I go home and stare at David Bowie and Amelia Blue. I want them to have sex. I want Amelia Blue to get pregnant. I don't know how fish have sex. I call my editor and ask him.

My editor says the female lays eggs on the floor of the tank. The male fertilizes the eggs. They have sex with no contact. Some fish can change gender.

Maybe both of my fish are girls. Maybe they're lesbians.

That night I have the twin dream again.

I see the car clearly this time. It's a silver Mercedes Benz like Manuel's.

Dr. Hill is right. I think I'm the one driving.

The body in the back seat looks exactly like me. Even the mole by my mouth.

She's not moving. If she's not dead, she's unconscious. I hope I didn't kill her. There's no blood. Maybe she's unconscious, or sleeping. But people don't sleep in that position. She looks dead. I hope I didn't kill her. I hope that's not why the police car is following me. I hear the siren. I don't think she's breathing.

I wake up in the middle of the night. I dunk my glass in the tank and drink some water. I cough a little, then I go back to bed.

The next morning, David Bowie is missing.

Fuck! David Bowie! My darling David Bowie! Where is he? What happened? Oh my God! Oh my fucking God!

Someone came into the house in the middle of the night, perhaps a burglar. Or maybe Mama took David Bowie because because…she was jealous. She was worried I loved David Bowie more than her. But Mama wouldn't kill a fish. Maybe she returned him to the pet store.

I hate Mama! I do, I do! I hate Mama so much I want the cord to snap! I no longer want to be one person, the same person! I want to be separated! I will never forgive Mama for this!

I yell at Mama. I tell her she is awful and I hate her and I want to go away, I want to move out, maybe live in my own apartment again. I cry and yell. I go into the kitchen, take a big knife and threaten to cut my throat.

Mama says I've gone crazy. She swears she didn't take or kill David Bowie. Mama begs me to take a tranquilizer. "Please, please," she says.

I am on the floor hyperventilating. My jaw is clamped down. Mama forces me to take a tranquilizer and drink some juice. She carries me to the couch. My small Mama carries me.

Fifteen minutes later, I feel a little better. I hear Mama on the phone with Dr. Hill. Then, Mama asks me nicely to put on my black dress pants and my ironed new blouse.

Mama and I are going to take the bus to see Dr. Hill. Papa has the car, so Mama and I are going to bus it. Mama holds my cold trembling hand. She begs me to try to stop twitching and look as normal as possible.

It's an hour bus ride to Dr. Hill's office. Mama talks and gently strokes my hand. This is soothing. I feel calm. But I can't talk back. My tongue is paralyzed and I'm drooling. Maybe people think I'm an epileptic. Poor Mama. It must be embarrassing.

How could I ever think Mama would take or kill David Bowie? I love Mama more than anyone. Mama and I are the same. There's no me without Mama. Mama is the best Mama in the world. I'm awful! I'm sick and crazy! Please forgive me, Mama. Please forgive me. What Mama dresses her thirty year old daughter, takes the bus with her, strokes her hand and wipes the dribble off her chin? Some Mamas would abandon their sick child, like Francis's mother abandoned him. I promise Mama to never yell at her again. I say I'm sorry. So sorry. She deserves a better daughter. But Mama says she wouldn't choose another daughter. She says I'm a good person and I'm smart. She says she's proud of me. She says she's glad I'm a writer, even though I use the word "fuck" a lot. This makes me laugh. And slobber more.

When we get to Dr. Hill's office we wait an hour. Mama talks to make the time pass quicker. She tells me how scared she was on the plane, that she thought the gay male flight attendant was hot, that she wanted the trip to be perfect, that she's sorry about her Mama and her sister. I tell Mama it's okay. If we hadn't gone, the street merchant wouldn't have told me to read *Veronika Decides To Die* by Paulo Coelho. And if I didn't read that I wouldn't have read *The Alchemist*. This is a nice conversation. I forget two hours ago I was ready to cut my throat with a kitchen knife.

Finally, Dr. Hill lets me in. He asks me how I'm doing, but he doesn't need to ask. One look at me and you'd know I was fucked. Totally fucked.

Dr. Hill asks Mama if I should be hospitalized. Mama says she will never let me be hospitalized ever again. She promised herself this the last time, when she could barely recognize her daughter.

Dr. Hill tells Mama to give me six tranquilizers every day for the next few days. Mama looks like she wants a second opinion but she says, "Yes. Thank you, Dr. Hill."

The next few days, I don't know when I'm awake or asleep. Everything is hazy. I'm driving. Then Mama's making me drink a glass of water with my tranquilizer. Then, my twin is dead in the back seat. Then, Mama's talking to me. Then, a police car is following me. Then, I'm watching T.V. Then, I'm looking in the rear view mirror.

Mama is so good. She feeds Amelia Blue while I'm incapacitated. I tell Mama it's of vital importance that Amelia Blue doesn't die. It was hard enough losing David Bowie. Losing Amelia Blue would kill me. Mama understands.

I tell Mama to ask Amelia Blue if she's depressed and tell me which direction she swims in. Mama says she swam to the right. I tell Mama to crumble an antidepressant and put it in the tank. Mama says yes but I have a feeling she won't do it.

One week later, Mama and I are at Dr. Hill's office again. I can barely keep my eyes open, but Dr. Hill says I'm better and I'm ready to go off the tranquilizers. He also says I should get some fresh air.

So every day for a week, Mama makes me walk with her for half an hour. I feel like an old dog whose hips are giving out. I think of my dead dog.

The following week, Dr. Hill says I should socialize more. I don't have any friends left, so I go see Sabrina. I find her lying on her bed and drinking. I think Sabrina is an alcoholic and a Satanist.

I don't want to sleep with her. I just want someone to get wasted with. I stole a bottle of pills from Mama's secret hiding place. She'll probably find out they're missing but I don't care.

Sabrina doesn't make an advances. Maybe she thinks I'm fat. Or maybe my cum tastes bad.

After a couple of hours of doing nothing, I decide to go home.

So, I'm walking down Whyte Avenue. That's when I see her. She looks exactly like me. Except she's wearing glasses. And she's pretty. But how can she look like me and be pretty? I'm not pretty.

She's talking to a man, a handsome man. Maybe he's her boyfriend. I pretend to be looking at the bus schedule. I love her glasses. Thick brown frames. They make her look so sophisticated. I wish I had glasses. She gives the man a hug and walks away. I follow her for a couple of blocks. Until she gets on the number 9 bus on 109 street. I look at my watch. It's 5:15.

I go home and stare at Amelia Blue. I say, "Amelia Blue, today I saw my doppelganger. Am I crazy?" Amelia Blue swims to the right.

I phone Sabrina. I tell her the same thing. Sabrina laughs and says it's all the pills and alcohol. I am probably hallucinating.

I tell Sabrina she must take the number 9 at 5:10 with me tomorrow.

Sabrina is lazy. She rarely leaves her room unless it's for alcohol or drugs. So I promise her a bottle of antipsychotics. I'm gonna have to lie to the pharmacist that I lost my meds again and they'll probably call Dr. Hill and Dr. Hill will be angry. Oh, well.

So the next day, Sabrina and I take the number 9. When my double gets on, I nudge Sabrina.

"You see!" I say.

But all Sabrina says is, "You guys have the same hair."

What the fuck!?! We have the same hair? This girl is the bloody spitting image of me, okay, except for the glasses. Sabrina is a fucking bitch! I hate her now!

"Maybe you've been doing too many drugs. You really should cut down. You're gonna end up like my boyfriend." Where is Sabrina's boyfriend anyway? Does he even exist? Or is he a figment of Sabrina's imagination? Maybe not only is Sabrina an alcoholic and a Satanist but a pathological liar!

"Look again!" I yell at her.

She says, "Yah, I guess…if you got glasses, were ten years younger, and ten pounds thinner."

Sabrina's right, I am fatter. Finally someone is being honest with me about my weight. I like Sabrina again now.

I ask Sabrina if she thinks this girl is my doppelganger. Sabrina says, "I don't know. Now, give me my drugs." I hand her the bottle.

When I get home I'm ecstatic. I say to Amelia Blue, "See, I wasn't hallucinating. I'm not crazy. The girl is real."

Mama knocks on my door. She says I've been going out too much. That I've been neglecting Amelia Blue.

That night, I dream I drive away from the police and stop the car. I open the car door. I lean over to move the body. The girl comes to life. She wraps her arms around me and kisses me deeply. So deeply, I feel my soul leave my body and enter hers.

The next time I see Dr. Hill I ask him if it's incestuous to be attracted to someone that looks like you. He says, "No".

I also ask Dr. Hill if he can prescribe me some diet pills. "Sure," he says and hands me a prescription. "Don't lose these."

The next day, I go to an optometrist. I pray he finds something wrong with my eyes. Even if it's minor, I'll get glasses.

Luckily, he finds some astigmatism.

I choose thick brown frames. When I put them on, I am transformed. I pretend I'm her, who's me.

Everyone compliments me on my glasses. Mama, Dr. Hill, Sabrina, Amelia Blue.

Every day, I think about my double. I wonder where she lives. If she has a husband or boyfriend or girlfriend.

Finally, I follow my double to her apartment building. She lives on the 8th floor.

She doesn't have any curtains. I can see her cooking, eating, watching T.V., talking on the phone.

I watch her from 5:30 to 9:30. Luckily no one calls the police. Picture me in a baseball cap, leaning against a tree, looking through binoculars, and taking photos with a camera with a zoom lens.

Sabrina's right, this girl must be around twenty. Maybe she's too young for me. Maybe I'm a wolf.

I go home and masturbate. I think of the girl that looks like me.

I dream the same dream. Except this time, the girl in the back seat opens her eyes.

> *Dr. H:* Are you feeling better?
> *A:* I saw my doppelganger.
> *Dr. H:* What do you mean?
> *A:* She looks exactly like me. I think she's the girl in the dream. The dead one. I think I killed her.

Dr. H: It's just a dream.

A: But what if it isn't? What if it's more?

Dr. H: Have you been taking too many pills?

A: Yes. I mean no.

Dr. H: My brother looks exactly like me except he's six inches taller.

A: You know what's really strange?

Dr. H: What?

A: She's pretty.

Dr. H: Why is that strange? You're pretty.

A: No, I'm not.

Dr. H: Yes, you are.

A: No. What if she's following me?

Dr. H: I thought you were following her.

A: Maybe she's going to kill me and steal my identity.

Dr. H: Or maybe she's just a girl that looks like you.

A: You haven't said anything about my glasses.

Dr. H: Didn't you always wear glasses?

A: No. I got them because they looked good on my doppelganger. Am I crazy for copying her?

Dr. H: When you start following her around with a camera, then I'll worry. See you next week?

A: Can I have a hug?

Dr. H: Sure.

A: Can you prescribe some diet pills?

Dr. H: Of course.

When I go over to Sabrina's, I talk about the girl. I feel so high. But I want to get even higher. So when Sabrina offers me cocaine, I don't turn it down.

Sabrina and I are sitting in a hot bath. It's innocent. We're just friends getting high together.

"Isn't it kind of incestuous? I mean, it's like fucking your twin, isn't it?"

"No."

"Whatever. Just don't let this be another X," Sabrina sounds just like Buddy.

I think I've fallen asleep. Everything is fuzzy. It feels like I'm not in my body anymore. I feel like I'm floating. I can see myself from up above. And I can see Sabrina. My body is convulsing and my nose is bleeding. There's blood in the water. But I can't feel anything. Sabrina isn't doing anything. She's just watching me bleed. My cord feels tight. It stretched all the way to L.A. but now it's tight. I don't want it to tear. Oh, please God, don't let it tear!

"Amelia, Amelia," a voice is calling.

I feel myself snap back into my body. Then, I feel a pair of arms around me. But they're not Sabrina's arms. These arms have tentacles.

My lungs are being filled with water. I'm drowning. A giant octopus is on top of me.

I'm in love. I don't want to die. I've wanted to die my entire life. But now I want to live. Desperately.

"Please let me go," I beg.

"Fuck you!" says the octopus.

When I open my eyes, I see Sabrina. She looks pissed off. "Holy shit, you swallowed some water. You snorted too much coke. I thought you were O.D.ing… You got to cut down. You're turning into a fucking addict."

I get my film developed.

I show Dr. Hill the photos.

A: See.

    Dr. H: She looks like you.

A: That's what I said.

    Dr. H: I never doubted you.

A: So, I'm not crazy?

    Dr. H: No, you're not.

A: Do you think she's my doppelganger?

    Dr. H: No.

A: What do you know about doppelgangers?

    Dr. H: Not much.

A: But you're German.

Dr. H: Half German.

A: I'm scared of dying. What if Buddy is right? What if there's nothing?

Dr. H: There's something.

A: Am I sick for wanting to have sex with her?

Dr. H: No.

A: Is it incestuous?

Dr. H: No. She's not your sister.

A: Is she too young?

Dr. H: Not if she's eighteen.

A: Do you think I'm a wolf?

Dr. H: What?

A: Never mind.

Dr. H: How are the diet pills?

A: Good.

Dr. H: You look thinner.

A: I'm still fat.

Dr. H: Are you experiencing any side effects?

A: Just shaky hands.

Dr. H: See, I told you the side effects would be mild. See you next week?

A: Okay. Can I have a hug?

Dr. H: Sure.

I don't tell Dr. Hill I'm hearing voices. I'm trying to ignore the voices.

So I do what a crazy person would do. I go up to the 8th floor and I knock on her door. When the girl who looks like me opens the door, she's wearing her glasses.

I say nothing. I don't need to say anything. It's like looking into the mirror.

This moment feels much longer than it is. Crazy me leans over and kisses her passionately. She kisses me back. We take off our clothes and make love on her bed. Now, I'm certain I love her.

I ask her, "Who are you?"

She says, "Angie."

I say, "No: Angel". And that is what I call her from then on.

I stop taking my meds. I don't need them any more. I'm happy.

The only problem is that I can't write. I sit in front of Angie's typewriter and stare at a blank sheet for hours. Like I'm staring at the white sky through the window of a plane.

But nothing comes to me. Oh well. At least I'm happy.

Mama cries and begs me not to stop my meds. "I don't want to lose you Amelia," she says.

"I'm not going anywhere," I reply.

A week later, I tell Mama I'm moving out, that I'm going to live with a friend. This makes Mama cry even more. By now Mama is crying all the time.

I think I've lost ten pounds. Angie and I look the same naked.

I've never been happier. But it seems no one is happy that I'm happy. Not Mama, Papa, my sisters, Dr. Hill, even Sabrina.

"You're pathetic. Don't come back 'til you're depressed again. I liked you better the other way."

A: This will be the last time.
  Dr. H: The last time for what?
A: The last time I see you.
  Dr. H: Why?
A: I don't need you anymore. I'm happy.
  Dr. H: I want you to be happy.
A: I don't need the pills either.
  Dr. H: Amelia, you're ill. It's very serious.
A: I'm cured.
  Dr. H: Why?
A: Love.
  Dr. H: Love can't cure what you have.
A: I'm happy.
  Dr. H: I strongly advise you not to go off the medication.

A: It's my decision.

   Dr. H: You could have another breakdown and have to be hospitalized. Think of your Mama.

A: I won't have another breakdown. It's different now. Can I have a good-bye hug?

   Dr. H: Sure.

A: Thank you, Dr. Hill.

   Dr. H: You can come back anytime.

A: Don't take this the wrong way, but I hope I never have to see you again.

   Angie: I love your glasses.

Amelia: They're the same as yours.

   Angie: I know. You're funny.

Amelia: No, I'm not.

   Angie: You're beautiful and funny and interesting.

Amelia: No, I'm not. But my Mama is.

   Angie: I would love to meet your Mama.

Amelia: How old are you?

   Angie: Eighteen. How old are you?

Amelia: Thirty.

   Angie: That's okay.

Amelia: Are you sure?

   Angie: Yes.

Amelia: I was raped.

   Angie: I want to kill him.

Amelia: Thank you. Do you want to go fishing?

   Angie: Fuck, yeah!

After eight months of living with Angel, eight months of bliss, Angel becomes quiet. I ask her what's wrong. She says she doesn't know.

I feel like she's keeping something from me. Like she has a secret. Maybe she's having an affair.

Angel works at a flower shop. While she's at work, I stay at the apartment and clean. She usually calls me at least three times a day. Then, one day she stops.

Usually when she comes home, we make love. But one day, she says she's too tired. I kiss her and start to take off her clothes. "Please don't," she says. Then, she goes to sleep.

The next day, she doesn't go to work.

Angie stays in bed for three days. I stare at her like I'm staring at my fish.

Mama phones me every day. She asks me if I want to go home. I say "No," but I'm tempted.

One day, Mama has bad news for me. She says Amelia Blue is dead. She thinks she died of loneliness. It then occurs to me that Mama might be lonely.

I call Dr. Hill and ask him what someone should do if someone they know has been in bed for three days and won't eat or even drink water.

Dr. Hill asks me if I want to go to the hospital. I say "No."

Amelia: What's wrong?

   Angie: It's burning me. It's like staring into the sun.

Amelia: Is it my fault?

   Angie: Yes.

Amelia: I'm sorry.

   Angie: I'm not.

Amelia: Do you want to read my poetry?

   Angie: Okay.

Amelia: You are my dearest darling fishy.

   Angie: What kind?

Amelia: A rainbow trout. I can't live without you.

   Angie: What if I die, Melly?

Amelia: I will bury you in Blueland.

   Angie: Why in Blueland?

Amelia: Because the most beautiful cemeteries are in Blueland.

   Angie: You're so romantic.

Amelia: I know nothing of love. Only what you've taught me.

Angie: You know too much. Kiss me.
Amelia: But I don't want to kill you.
   Angie: It's too late.

It's the eighth day and Angel isn't moving. I check to see if she's breathing. She is. "Get up," I say. No movement.

"Get the fuck up!" I yell. Nothing.

"You fucking stupid cow! I fucking hate you! Get up! You're driving me fucking crazy!" I say.

I take a pillow and beat her with it.

"What's the matter with you?"

She mumbles something. I tell her to say it again.

"I'm depressed," she says.

I find a bottle of pills I kept just in case. I beg her to take a couple with some water. She says "No."

That night, I have my usual dream.

This time, when I open the car door, and my double comes to life, I strangle her. I kill her. She's dead, and I'm glad.

I wake up in pain. There's blood on the sheets. Is it menstrual blood? No; I've cut my leg.

There's a knife, a big fucking knife in the bed. Angie must've taken it from the kitchen.

Maybe this isn't a premonition. Maybe it's a dream. Just electrical impulses being fired randomly in the brain. But I'm not going to take a chance. One of us could end up dead.

I pack my bags and leave.

Mama is so happy when she sees me. She looks awful. I've never seen her look so awful.

Mama kisses me a thousand times and says, "Amelia Blue's come back to me. Thank God."

Mama asks me if she can get me anything, anything at all. I say, "Yes, my medication."

Mama smiles.

Then she notices I'm bleeding. Mama shrieks.

Mama pours some alcohol over my wound, finds some fishing wire, and sews some stitches.

"They feel like fish scales," I say.

The next day, I see Dr. Hill.

He hugs me, says he's missed me. I tell him I missed him too.

"Love wasn't enough, was it?"

"No," I say.

Then, I go to Sabrina's. I tell her I left Angie, that all she did was sleep, that I wished she was dead.

Sabrina is amused.

We smoke some pot and get drunk.

I seduce her.

I haven't spoken to Angie for two weeks.

Then she phones me. She says I left a book behind, *The Bell Jar*.

I go over to her apartment. She's in her pajamas. Her hair is uncombed and she stinks. She looks fucked. Totally fucked.

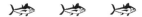

Angie: Why did you leave?

Amelia: It was like being with me.

Angie: You want all the good stuff, but you have to take the bad with the good.

Amelia: You disgust me.

Angie: Because I'm depressed?

Amelia: Please take a shower and put on something nice. I want you to take these pills. And I want you to see someone. He's very nice.

Angie: No.

Amelia: You're ill.

Angie: Give me another chance. It'll be different.

Amelia: I need to go home. My Mama needs me.

    Angie: Will you ever come see me again?

Amelia: I don't know.

    Angie: I had this dream. This girl who looks like me is driving. The police are following her car. I'm in the back seat. Dead.

Amelia: It's just a dream. Goodbye.

I go back to say I'm sorry. I hear screams from below. Angie isn't in bed. I go to the balcony and look down to see where the noise is coming from. A group of people are standing around a body. A dead body in a pool of blood on the concrete.

THE END

About the Author

Writer/composer/director Zhauna Alexander's previous work includes *Amelia's Aquarium* (Slipstream Books, 1999), three plays (*Zeno's Deli, Cake*, and *Pigs*), three short films (*Smear, The Good Samaritan, apples & oranges*) and numerous songs. Her plays have enjoyed sold-out houses at the *Edmonton Fringe Theatre Festival* and her film work has garnered awards at the *Local Heroes Film Festival*. Ms. Alexander lives in St. Albert, Alberta.

Also Available from Slipstream Books

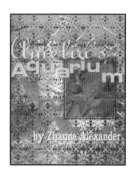

Amelia's Aquarium
by Zhauna Alexander
ISBN 1-895836-66-2

Amelia Blue has been dealt a difficult hand by Fate: manic-depressive, bisexual, obsessive-compulsive and unlucky in love. Poet Zhauna Alexander invites you to shuffle the cards and see what difference you can make to Amelia's life. Spare, funny and beautifully presented as a deck of 64 cards in a colourful box, *Amelia's Aquarium* is an ideal gift.

The Edmonton Queen *by Darrin Hagen* ISBN 1-895836-46-8
A compelling memoir of urban prairie nightlife, The Edmonton Queen follows a dynasty of drag queens who reigned over the celebrities and denizens of Edmonton's 1980's party culture. Illustrated with 88 photographs. Developed from the Sterling Award-winning play.

Neurotic Erotica *by Timothy J. Anderson* ISBN 1-895836-18-2
The book that sparked a crusade by Alberta Report against arts funding in Alberta. A thoughtful exploration of the sources of desire, the relationship between poetry and truth, and a fun read. Foreword by feminist psychologist Robyn Mott and cover art by internationally acclaimed artist Evergon.

My Tongue All Thumbs *by Gerry Dotto* ISBN 1-895836-47-6
For lovers of concrete poetry, visual puns, and the just plain weird. Gerry Dotto's pen and lens present brain teasers, rib ticklers, and a good dollop of wry humour.

Vajolin/Violin *by Marijan Megla* ISBN 1-895836-60-3
Tales of Romany life by the irrepressible Croatian-Canadian Marijan Megla. Written in phonetic English ("Meglish"), you can sound it out for the flavour of the author's voice, or read the more standard English version translated by Reg Silvester.

Gypsy Messenger *by Marijan Megla and Sima Khorrami* ISBN 1-895836-82-4
Stunning black and white photographs of gypsy life accompanied by evocative poetry, with "Meglish" and English lines side-by-side. This book makes a welcome gift for either the photography or poetry afficionado.

Visit our website: www.bookscollective.com or e-mail us at: slipstream@bookscollective.com